Arden swallowed, kn ~~question had nothing~~ **...** addresses **or phone books.**

Garrett was asking if his suspicions were accurate, and she couldn't bring herself to answer. There was a huge difference between not tracking down a man to deliver life-altering news he probably didn't want to hear and actually lying to his face.

He took a step closer. "You seemed so startled to see me the other day. Terrified, as a matter of fact."

Feeling cornered, she took deep breaths, trying to lower her elevated blood pressure.

"Maybe I'm completely off base," he continued, "but extenuating circumstances have made me more distrustful than I used to be. If I'm wrong, you can laugh at me or indignantly cuss me out. But tell me the truth, Arden. Are you carrying my child?"

Dear Reader,

I first visited Colorado when I was a teenager and have made numerous trips since then. It's a beautiful state full of wonderful communities, the perfect setting for my new trilogy, The Colorado Cades.

The Cade siblings, two brothers and the younger sister they raised after their parents' deaths, really tugged at my heart. It's not easy to find happiness when you've experienced great loss—but with hope and faith, it is possible.

On an evening when she needed to escape grief and nostalgia, Arden Cade had an uncharacteristic one-night stand with cowboy Garrett Frost, an out-of-towner visiting Cielo Peak. She never expected to see him again...and she certainly didn't expect to become pregnant from their night together!

Six months later, after receiving some shocking news of his own, Garrett returns to Cielo Peak to stay with a friend while making difficult decisions. When Garrett sees Arden, two things are quickly evident—the chemistry between them is as potent as ever. And she's been keeping an unforgivable secret.

I'm hard at work on the next two books in the trilogy. For behind-the-scenes looks at my process and anecdotes about the writing life, follow me on Twitter or like me on Facebook. I love interacting with readers!

Happy reading,

Tanya

HER SECRET, HIS BABY

—

TANYA MICHAELS

HARLEQUIN® AMERICAN ROMANCE®

Recycling programs
for this product may
not exist in your area.

ISBN-13: 978-0-373-75467-0

HER SECRET, HIS BABY

Printed in U.S.A.

HARLEQUIN®
www.Harlequin.com

ABOUT THE AUTHOR

Three-time RITA® Award nominee Tanya Michaels writes about what she knows—community, family and lasting love! Her books, praised for their poignancy and humor, have received honors such as a Booksellers' Best Bet Award, a Maggie Award of Excellence and multiple readers' choice awards. She was also a 2010 *RT Book Reviews* nominee for Career Achievement in Category Romance. Tanya is an active member of Romance Writers of America and a frequent public speaker, presenting workshops to educate and encourage aspiring writers. She lives outside Atlanta with her very supportive husband, two highly imaginative children and a household of quirky pets, including a cat who thinks she's a dog and a bichon frise who thinks she's the center of the universe.

Books by Tanya Michaels

HARLEQUIN AMERICAN ROMANCE
1170—TROUBLE IN TENNESSEE
1185—THE PERFECT TREE
    "Tanner and Baum"
1203—AN UNLIKELY MOMMY
1225—A DAD FOR HER TWINS
1235—MISTLETOE BABY*
1255—MISTLETOE CINDERELLA*
1270—MISTLETOE MOMMY*
1279—MISTLETOE HERO*
1311—THE BEST MAN IN TEXAS
1321—TEXAS BABY
1343—HIS VALENTINE SURPRISE
1368—A MOTHER'S HOMECOMING
1388—CLAIMED BY A COWBOY**
1399—TAMED BY A TEXAN**
1419—RESCUED BY A RANGER**
1438—MY COWBOY VALENTINE
    "Hill Country Cupid"

*4 Seasons in Mistletoe
**Hill Country Heroes

Dedicated with gratitude to Barbara Dunlop—
wonderful author, friend and dinner companion.

Chapter One

Never in her twenty-five years had Arden Cade done anything so rash. *What was I thinking?* Although she usually woke in gradual, disoriented stages, this morning she was instantly alert, hoping to discover the previous night had been a dream—a vivid, thoroughly sensual dream.

But there was no disputing the muscular arm across her midsection or the lingering satisfaction in her body.

Physically, she was more relaxed than she'd been in nearly a year, her loose limbs at odds with her racing thoughts. Her first impulse was to bolt from the bed, putting distance between herself and the still-sleeping cowboy. She hesitated, not wanting to wake Garrett before she'd had a chance to gather her composure. Besides, his body heat and the steady rumble of his breathing were soothing. Beckoning. It was so tempting to snuggle closer beneath the sheets and—

Don't you learn?

Cuddling into his heat was what had landed her in this situation. But she'd been cold for so long. She'd needed to feel something other than suffocating grief. If only yesterday hadn't been the ninth of March.... What the hell had made her think scheduling a photography job would keep her too busy to mourn?

Memories of the night before flooded her—the despair that had gaped like a chasm, the encounter with a charming stranger, the reckless bliss she'd found in his arms.

"If you don't mind my saying so, ma'am, people usually look happier at wedding receptions." The man's teasing tone was deep and rich, unexpectedly warming her.

She had to tilt her head to meet his clear gray eyes. Knowing her clients deserved better than a photographer who depressed the guests, she struggled for a light tone as she gestured toward the crowded dance floor. "I was feeling sorry for myself because I'm not out there," she lied. "I love to dance."

A slow grin stole over his face, making him even more attractive. As the younger sister of two ridiculously good-looking brothers, Arden didn't impress easily, but this man made her pulse quicken.

"I'd be happy to oblige," he offered. "I realize you're working, but I have some pull with the groom. Hugh was my best friend in high school."

His casual words pierced her. Arden had kept the same best friend from preschool into adulthood, rejoicing three and a half years ago when the sister of her heart married Arden's oldest brother and became her sister-in-law. This was the first March 9—Natalie's birthday—since the car accident that had killed Natalie and her toddler son, the first March 9 in over two decades Arden hadn't spent with her friend.

"Rain check," she'd managed to respond, abandoning the stranger to snap shots of the twirling flower girl.

After the reception ended, Arden should have gone home, but facing her dark, empty apartment seemed unbearable. She packed her equipment, then sat in the hotel bar while ice melted in her untouched whiskey. Time passed with excruciating slowness.

Then Garrett Frost walked in, his earlier suit replaced with a casual button-down shirt and a pair of dark jeans that somehow made him even more devastatingly handsome.

"I'd offer to buy you a drink, but..." He raised one jet-black eyebrow at the liquor she was clearly ignoring.

"Guess I wasn't thirsty, after all."

Their gazes locked, and she wished she had a camera in hand to capture his mesmerizing eyes. He's beautiful. *Sculpted cheekbones, full mouth—*

"If you're gonna look at me like that," he'd drawled softly, "it's only fair you tell me your name."

"Arden. Arden Cade."

He extended his hand. "You still want that dance, Arden Cade?"

She'd accepted. Sometimes what a woman needed most in the world was to be held....

"Mornin'." Tinged with sleep, Garrett's voice now was every bit as compelling as it had been last night—when he'd breathed her name as he slid into her.

Arden! Focus! Last night's impulsiveness was one thing. She'd been emotionally raw, had needed to feel alive in some primal way. But she couldn't rationalize a repeat performance. She'd had only two sexual partners before, and they'd both been serious boyfriends.

She scrambled for the edge of the bed, trying to secure the sheet around her as she moved. "Yes, it is. Morning, I mean. Time for me to go."

"Don't hurry on my account." He lay back on his pillow, grinning at her in utter contentment. His appeal was more than physical good looks. She was drawn to his easy confidence, how comfortable he seemed in his own skin.

"Checkout's not 'til noon," he continued. "Thought I might order us an obscenely large breakfast from room service. I'm starvin'."

So was she, Arden realized. After months of being numb, of having no appetite whatsoever, the hunger felt both foreign and exhilarating. "I could eat," she blurted.

"Good. I'm gonna hop in the shower, then we can look at the menu. I'll only be a minute. Unless you want to join me?" He gave her another of those lazy smiles that left her dizzy. Garrett made love the way he smiled. Completely and thoroughly, in seemingly no rush.

"N-no." She ducked her head so that her long dark hair curtained her face. It was probably bad manners to look appalled at the thought of being naked with a man who had rocked your world mere hours ago. "I'll, uh, wait."

He sauntered across the room nude, and Arden resisted the urge to sneak a final glance. Not that her resistance held for long. He was male perfection.

And he'd been exactly what she'd needed last night. As unplanned and perhaps unwise as her actions had been, she had to admit she felt…lighter. She could almost hear Natalie's mischievous voice in her head. *Damn, girl, you really know how to celebrate a birthday.*

Arden squeezed her eyes shut. *I miss you, Nat.* That ache might never go away, but it was time Arden stopped letting it drag her down like a malevolent anchor. Natalie would have hated how listless she'd become.

The sound of the shower in the adjoining bathroom pulled Arden from her reverie. Garrett had claimed he'd be back in a minute. What was she going to say to him? All she really knew about him was that his family owned a cattle ranch several hours south of Cielo Peak and that he'd come to town for the Connors' wedding. She didn't know how to be glib about what they'd shared, and she didn't want to burden him with a heavy emotional explanation about the losses she and her brothers had endured. Wouldn't the simplest solution be to leave now, without an awkward goodbye?

She zipped her wrinkled dress, trying not to think about how she'd look to anyone she passed in the lobby. Cielo Peak attracted plenty of tourists, especially during the Colorado ski season, but there were fewer than fifteen hundred year-round citizens. The Cades were well known in the community; gossip about Arden hooking up with a guest at an event she covered would not enhance her professional reputation.

Her hand was already on the door when she stopped abruptly, recalling how Garrett had touched her the night before, his maddening tenderness. He'd made her nearly mindless with desire, and it had been the first time in months the pain had receded. Among her many conflicted feelings this morning was gratitude. He would never truly understand how much he'd given her, but she didn't want him to think she regretted being with him.

She grabbed the pen and notepad that bore the hotel logo and scribbled a quick note. It wasn't much, but it helped ease her conscience.

Garrett, thank you for last night. It was...

A barrage of words filled her mind, none of them adequate. Suddenly, the water stopped in the bathroom. Adrenaline coursed through her. She crossed out the last two words and wrote simply *I'll never forget you.*

Chapter Two

Six months later

Justin Cade shuddered at the brochures on the kitchen table. "I will paint nursery walls, I will assemble the crib, I might be wheeled into a few hours of babysitting once the peanut is born, but no way in hell am I attending birth classes with you." Then he flashed his trademark grin, a mischievous gleam in his blue-green eyes. "Unless you think there will be a lot of single women attending?"

Arden ignored the question. He'd already proven he wasn't comfortable dating a single mom. Justin, the middle Cade sibling, had raised casual dating to an art form and steered clear of women with complicated lives. The ski patrolman didn't like being stuck in a relationship any more than he liked being stuck indoors.

Thank God he's a more dependable brother than he is a boyfriend. "I didn't pull out the brochures to show you, dummy. I'm going to ask Layla to be my labor coach. She's coming over for dinner in a couple of hours."

Back in June, when the "first trimester" nausea Arden had thought would disappear actually intensified, she'd hired a temporary assistant to keep up with the administrative side of the studio. High school Spanish teacher Layla Green had been happy to make some extra money over the summer. The women's friendship continued to grow even though Layla had quit to prepare for the new school year.

"Layla, huh?" Justin crossed the small kitchen to pour another glass of iced tea. He frequently joked that the desert theme of her red-and-yellow kitchen made him extra thirsty. "She's good people. Cute, too."

"Hey! We've talked about this. You are not allowed to date my friends. Your one-hit-wonder approach to relationships would make things awkward for everyone. I was even a bit nervous when Natalie…" She trailed off, the memories bittersweet.

The sharp sting of missing her best friend had lessened over time. As Arden progressed through the trimesters, she found herself thinking of Natalie as a kind of guardian angel for her and the unborn baby. After losing so many loved ones in her life, it seemed cosmically fitting that Arden had conceived on Nat's birthday.

"You wondered if it would hurt your friendship when Natalie and Colin first started dating?" Justin asked. "To be honest, I thought the age difference would be a problem, that they wouldn't have enough in common for it to be long-lasting. But she made him damn happy."

While Arden was finally healing after the deaths of her sister-in-law and young nephew, Colin had withdrawn further. Not only had he taken a sabbatical from his job as a large-animal vet, but he'd also recently announced that he was putting his house up for sale.

She leaned an elbow on the table, propping her chin on her fist. "I'm really worried about him."

"Colin will be okay." But the way Justin avoided her gaze proved he was equally concerned. "He's always okay. He's the one who holds us together."

Their mother had died the winter Arden was in kindergarten, their father a few years later. Although a maiden aunt had come to live with them, it had been Colin who had essentially raised his younger brother and sister. He'd been so strong. But this most recent shattering loss—burying his wife and child? It seemed as if something inside him had broken beyond repair.

Justin dropped down next to Arden's chair, squeezing her shoulder. "He *will* be okay. Maybe selling the house will help him let go, give him a chance to move forward with his life."

Arden placed her hands over her distended abdomen. "Do you think this makes it harder, my having a baby? I'm sure it reminds him of Danny." Her voice caught on her nephew's name. He'd been a wide-eyed, soft-spoken toddler with an unexpectedly raucous belly laugh. His deep laugh had caused double takes in public, usually eliciting chuckles in response.

"If you're happy about Peanut, then we are happy for you," Justin said firmly. "But if you want to offer Colin some kind of distraction, I'm sure he'd be eager to track down the jerk who knocked you—"

"Justin!"

"The jerk responsible for your being in a blessed family way."

"He wasn't a jerk. He was…" A gift. Even after six months, she vividly recalled Garrett's ability to make her temporarily forget everything else in the world, the power of his touch.

Justin recoiled with a grimace. "Seeing that look on my little sister's face is disturbing as hell. You sure you won't tell us who he is so we can punch his lights out?"

"He doesn't live anywhere near here." Thank God. Most of the locals hadn't been brazen enough to ask outright who the father was, but the mystery had caused whispers behind her back. Some of the teachers in the district had begged Layla for information, but Arden— who'd shared only the vaguest details—had sworn her to secrecy. The first time Arden had encountered Hugh Connor in town after her pregnancy began to show, she'd held her breath, wondering if Garrett had ever mentioned their night together to his friend. But Hugh had merely asked for a business card because he planned to recommend her to a business colleague looking for a good photographer.

Meanwhile, Garrett lived in a different region of the state, on a ranch he'd told her had been in his family for generations. He had deep roots there. Maybe even a girlfriend by now. Arden didn't plan to repay the kindness he'd done her by upending his existence. They'd used birth control during their night together, and the news that it had failed would most likely be an unwelcome shock.

It had taken her weeks to process the news that she was expecting, but she knew firsthand that life was precious. She chose to see conceiving this baby as a miracle. *Her* miracle.

Garrett Frost held his parents in the highest regard. An only child, he worked alongside his father running the Double F Ranch and was impressed with the man's drive and integrity. Garrett's mother, the one who'd spent many afternoons giving him advice in their kitchen while she baked, had always been wise and articulate. So why, today, had Caroline Frost lost the ability to string together a coherent sentence? Ever since the restaurant hostess had seated Garrett and Caroline at a small booth, she'd been spluttering disjointed, half-finished thoughts.

"Breathe, Momma." He took the breadbasket out of her hand. As jittery as she was, she was about to send the rolls flying to the floor. He gave her a cajoling smile. "You wanna tell me why you're as nervous as a kitten in a dog pound?"

Her gray eyes clouded with worry. "You've always hated surprises," she muttered. "Not that it's your fault if you take this badly! Anyone would…. I don't— Lord, I've messed this up before I even started. But I don't know how to make it better. Easier to hear."

Okay. Now *he* was nervous. Garrett waved away the approaching waitress. Something was very wrong. He doubted his mom wanted an audience for whatever she needed to explain. Although, if she had something personal and difficult to tell him, why had she suggested going to a restaurant?

They could have easily had a conversation in his parents' main house or in the luxurious cabin Garrett had built on the back forty. The most logical explanation for her dragging him this far from home was so they could speak freely without any risk of his father overhearing. Was something wrong with him? Long, arduous days of ranch work could take a toll, and Brandon wasn't getting any younger. But his father was direct to a fault. If there was bad news to be delivered, he would have told Garrett himself, not delegated the job to someone else.

"Momma, is everything all right with you?" he asked slowly. "Is there some irregular test result or something I should know about?"

"With me? I'm fit as a fiddle." But she'd gone completely pale.

"Oh, God. Then it *is* Dad?"

Caroline did something he hadn't witnessed since the day of his high school graduation. She burst into tears. "No. And y-yes. Your father's quite ill. B-but it's not wh-wh-what you think." Taking deep gulping breaths, she clutched the edge of the table in a visible effort to regain her composure. "I'm so sorry. Brandon isn't your father."

GARRETT PUNCHED UP the volume on the music in his truck, but it was pointless. Not even the loudest rock and roll could drown out his tumultuous thoughts. He pounded his fist on the steering wheel, rage rising in him like a dark tide. Tangible enough to drown him.

For the first day after his mother's avalanche of revelations, he'd been too numb to feel anything. Once emotion rushed in, he'd realized he had to get away from the ranch. Away from her. She'd had thirty years to tell the truth but had never said a word—not to him and not to the man he'd always believed was his father. Now she'd made Garrett an unwilling accomplice in keeping her adulterous secret. "I swear it was only the one time," she'd sobbed. "A lifetime ago. Confessing my sins to Brandon might ease my conscience, but why wound him like that?"

Her single indiscretion had been with a longtime family friend, recently hospitalized Will Harlow. Complications from Will's diabetes had irreparably damaged his kidneys. Though his condition was currently stable, renal failure was inevitable. Without a kidney transplant, his prognosis was grim. Caroline insisted they couldn't tell Brandon now. "If Will died with animosity between them, your father would never forgive himself!"

How had Brandon remained oblivious to the truth for all these years? He was an intuitive man. Certainly perceptive enough that he would notice the awful tension between his wife and son. So Garrett impulsively announced that he was spending Labor Day weekend with Hugh Connor.

"I don't know exactly when I'll be back," Garrett had warned his dad. "With calving season behind us and time before we need to make winter preparations, can you spare me?"

Brandon had readily agreed that he and their hired hands could cover everything, adding that Garrett didn't seem himself and maybe a week of R & R was just what the doctor ordered. Garrett's sole motivation had been escape; he hadn't consciously chosen Cielo Peak as his destination. Had he named the town because he knew it wouldn't sound suspicious, his visiting an old friend?

Or was he lured by the heated memories of a glorious night spent with Arden Cade?

Their encounter had left such an impression it was haunting. She appeared in his dreams at random intervals. He'd developed a fondness for brunettes and had caught himself unintentionally comparing a date to her. Over the summer, while packing for an annual weekend with some cousins, he'd discovered Arden's note stuck to the lining of his suitcase. *I'll never forget you.* Was that sentiment invitation enough to look her up while he was in town?

She was a beautiful woman, and over six months had passed. Even if she still resided in Cielo Peak, there was likely a man in her life. Unless, like Garrett, she was between relationships? Maybe he could casually broach the subject with Hugh.

When Garrett had phoned his friend, it had been to ask for suggestions of a not-too-touristy rental cabin that wouldn't already be booked for the holiday weekend. He hadn't actually planned to stay with Hugh and Darcy, who were practically newlyweds. Learning of his mom's infidelity had soured Garrett's opinion of wedded bliss, and he doubted he'd be great company. But Hugh was stubborn. Besides, Garrett secretly questioned whether too much time alone with his thoughts was healthy. After all, he was having trouble surviving just the drive, battered by emotional debris from Caroline's bombshell.

He fiddled with the radio dials again, trading his MP3 playlist for a radio station. A twangy singer with a guitar droned on about his misfortunes. *You think* you *have problems, pal?*

Garrett faced not only bitter disillusionment about the woman who raised him and unwilling participation in her long-term deception, but also a monumental medical decision.

Despite Caroline's emphatic vows that her fling with Will was an isolated event, that they didn't harbor any romantic feelings for each other, the man had never fallen in love with anyone else. He'd remained a bachelor with no children. Garrett was his best hope for a close match and voluntary organ donation, which would drastically shorten the wait.

"I know you need to think about this," his mother had told him. "No one wants you to rush a decision." But they both knew Will didn't have forever.

If Garrett agreed, would he feel as if he were betraying his father? If he said no, was it the same as sentencing a man to die?

He was mired in anger and pain and confusion. Little wonder, then, that his mind kept turning to that night he'd shared with Arden, the perfect satisfaction he'd experienced. Right now, it was difficult to imagine he'd ever feel that purely happy again.

Chapter Three

Arden sighed wistfully at the seafood counter. "I miss shrimp."

"Throw some in." Justin indicated the grocery cart he was pushing for her. "How about this? I'll pay if you'll cook." Even with the holiday sales price, it was a generous offer. Since ski season hadn't started, he was scraping by on a reduced off-season salary working for a local ambulance service.

After a moment of letting herself be tempted, she shook her head. "Nah, I've read warnings that pregnant women should avoid shellfish. Skipping them completely might be overreacting, but I really want to do this right, you know?"

She rarely missed her mom, having been so young when Rebecca Cade died, but she sure could use a woman who'd experienced the wonder and worry of impending motherhood. Her only living aunt who'd had children was well over sixty, her memories of pregnancy and childbirth hazy and outdated. Arden hesitated to take advice from a woman who'd chain-smoked and enjoyed cocktail hour through all three trimesters. Cousin Rick never had seemed quite right in the head.

Arden changed the subject, eyeing her brother curiously. "You know, you've been hanging around an awful lot lately. Does this sudden fascination with helping me have anything to do with missing Elisabeth?" Though Justin's relationships never lasted long, Arden thought she'd sensed genuine regret after his most recent breakup—and not only because he missed the job as hiking guide and first-aid administrator at the lodge Elisabeth's family owned.

"What? No. I barely think about her. *You're* the one who keeps bringing her up!"

I am? Arden wracked her brain, trying to recall the last time she'd mentioned Elisabeth Donnelly.

"I'm giving up my Sunday afternoon because you shouldn't be lifting things," he added virtuously. "What would you have done if I hadn't been here to grab the pallet of bottled water?"

"Um, asked any one of the numerous stock boys for assistance?"

He shoved a hand through his dark brown hair. "Humor me, okay? I have two siblings I care the world about, and one of them, I don't have a clue how to help."

So he was overcompensating by lending a hand with her menial errands? That she could believe.

"Besides," Justin drawled, "being such a good brother makes me look all sensitive and whatever to any single ladies we encounter. Major attraction points."

On behalf of women everywhere, she socked him in the shoulder. "You go to the freezer section and get us an enormous tub of vanilla ice cream. I'll grab caramel and chocolate syrup."

"And some straw—"

"Of course strawberry syrup for you," she added.

There was no accounting for taste. "Then we'll need bananas. Meet me in produce, okay? I'll make chef salads for dinner and sundaes for dessert."

He turned to go, then hesitated. "Should we invite Colin to join us? Granted, he's not exactly Mr. Fun these days, but..."

"I'll call him," Arden promised. "But you know he'll probably decline. Again."

"If the situation were reversed, he wouldn't give up on either of us. Maybe it would help if you pick up some of those minimarshmallows for the sundaes. He's a sucker for those."

"Minimarshmallows?" she echoed skeptically. "That's our plan?"

Justin shrugged. "Hey, we all have our weaknesses."

GARRETT WHEELED THE shopping cart into the produce section, absently navigating as he consulted Darcy's grocery list. He'd asked her to let him do the supermarket run as a way to pay the Connors back for room and board. It was more diplomatic than saying he needed a break from the doting couple.

Conversation between Garrett and Hugh had been uncharacteristically stilted. Garrett wanted to confide in his friend but hadn't quite worked up the courage. It felt disloyal to tell anyone what Caroline had done, and it rocked Garrett's sense of identity to admit Brandon wasn't his father. He'd never said the words aloud, and they were harder than he'd expected.

The other potential topic of discussion Garrett wrestled with was Arden Cade. He'd started to ask about her half a dozen times, but stopped himself. After their intimate night together, she'd left without saying good-bye. That seemed like a strong indicator that she wasn't expecting to see him again.

Blinking, Garrett whipped his head around in a double take. A dark-haired woman in his peripheral vision had triggered his notice. *You're pitiful.* Just because he'd been thinking of Arden, now random shoppers looked like her?

Or, maybe… Could it actually *be* Arden? The long fall of shiny brown hair was familiar. He could recall its silky texture between his fingers. Given the crappy week he was having, had fate decided it owed him a favor? He hadn't figured out a casual way to look her up, but he couldn't be blamed for a chance encounter.

Steering toward her, he asked hopefully, "Arden?"

"Yes?" She smiled over her shoulder but froze in recognition, his name on her lips so soft he saw it rather than heard it. "Garrett."

He couldn't believe she was here—and even more beautiful than he remembered. Her cheeks were rosy, her aquamarine eyes bright and lively. He couldn't recall noticing a woman's skin before, but Arden's creamy complexion beckoned him to touch her.

Garrett realized two things at once: he was staring, and she didn't look happy to see him. Then he came up alongside her, getting his first real look at her profile, and had a startling third revelation. Arden Cade was pregnant.

It wasn't immediately obvious until one saw her stomach. She seemed to be carrying the baby completely in front. From behind, other than the curve of her hips, there hadn't been— Good Lord. He was ogling a pregnant woman.

He swallowed. "So. How've you been?" He punctuated his question with a wry glance at her abdomen. He knew nothing about pregnancy. His understanding was that women didn't show for a few weeks, although Arden was slim enough that perhaps it was more obvious on her than it would have been on someone else. He had no real sense of whether she was four months along or eight.

That was a sobering thought. Was there a chance she'd already been carrying when they'd made love? The possibility upset him beyond any rational justification.

"I, uh…" Her eyes cut to the side, as if she were seeking help. Or scoping exit routes. "It's good to see you."

Wow, are you a bad liar, sweetheart. "You're obviously busy." He gestured to the bananas she'd been perusing. "I won't keep you. I'm staying in town with the Connors for a few days, and when I saw you there, I thought I'd say hi."

The tension in her shoulders eased fractionally. "Hi." She managed a smile, but it didn't reach her eyes.

"Arden? Is there a problem here?" A broad-shouldered man approached, his tone possessive as he practically rammed his cart between Arden and Garrett. He was a tall son of a gun, even had an inch or two of height on Garrett.

"No problem, Justin. Except that I'm…feeling sick." Her progressively ashen color backed up her claim. She dropped the produce bag she'd been holding into the cart. "Get me home. I can come back later for anything we missed."

"Don't be ridiculous. *I'll* come back." When he glanced at her, Justin's features softened. But the glare he aimed at Garrett was flinty with suspicion.

Garrett's stomach dropped. He'd known there was a good chance Arden would be involved with someone. So why was his disappointment at being right so keenly bitter?

Wait a minute. His eyes narrowed, and he met Justin's unblinking stare. Those blue-green eyes were a lot like Arden's. And the thick brown hair they both shared? Arden's was streaked with honey and gold, while the man's was more like coffee grounds, but the resemblance was unmistakable.

A broad grin stretched across Garrett's face. "Is this your brother?"

"Damn right." The man took a step forward. "And *you* are…?"

"Justin, please." Arden's voice trembled. "I have to get out of here."

"Right. Sorry. Let's go."

With a hasty, departing wave from Arden, they were gone. Garrett stood there, bemused.

Had she truly been unhappy to see him, or did her not feeling well explain her behavior and the grimace she'd tried to cover? At first, he'd thought her skittish demeanor was due to the awkwardness of running into a fling while her significant other was nearby, but that wasn't the case. Maybe he'd misread the situation entirely.

But as he began piling groceries into the buggy, he

conjured her face again. He could have sworn the emotion he'd seen in her eyes was…fear. Why on earth would Arden be scared of him?

"GREAT DINNER," GARRETT complimented his hostess. Personally, he'd been too preoccupied to taste a bite of the meal, but Hugh had wolfed down his roast beef with gusto, so Garrett felt reasonably sure of his statement.

Darcy Connor, Hugh's pretty blonde wife, beamed from across the kitchen table. Her gregarious nature seemed at odds with the cliché image of a part-time librarian. "Lavish praise, doing the shopping for me— when word gets out about you, my single girlfriends are going to be lining up at the front door."

"Since you cooked, we can do the dishes," Hugh volunteered.

"Another time." She shooed them out of the kitchen. "Garrett just got here yesterday. You still have lots of catching up to do."

"Isn't she terrific?" Hugh asked adoringly as they relocated to the living room. He grabbed a television remote from the side pocket in his recliner, flipping through channels until he found a college football game. "If you'd told me when I was a freckled, fifteen-year-old comic book collector that I could get a woman like that to marry me…"

Garrett snorted. "You were also six feet tall and the team quarterback." His auburn-haired friend might well have freckles and an interest in superheroes, but he hadn't spent his teenage years lonely. "As I recall, you went to senior proms at three separate high schools."

Hugh grinned. "Did I? Before Darcy, it's all a blur.

What about you, man? You had a pretty active social life, too. I was surprised you didn't bring anyone to the wedding."

Boy, would that night have ended differently. A month prior to the wedding, he'd been dating a woman he'd planned to take to the ceremony, but they'd ended things when she got a job offer that took her to the east coast.

"Speaking of your wedding," Garrett said with studied nonchalance, "I never got to see how the photos turned out. Isn't there an album or something?"

"Darcy," he called to his wife, "you have a willing victim here. Garrett asked to see wedding pictures." Turning back to Garrett, he added, "Narrating our photos is one of her favorite hobbies, up there with bird-watching and snowboarding. I warn you, the collection is massive. There's the professional album our photographer put together, then the one Darcy crammed full of everything from wedding shower pics to the honeymoon."

"I remember the photographer," Garrett said. Understatement of the year—she was seared into his memory like a brand. "Arden, right?"

Hugh smirked. "Why, you looking for a photographer? Maybe planning to have some of those glamorized portraits done? You'd look pretty spiffy in a sequined cowboy hat."

"I think I ran into her at the grocery store earlier. The woman I saw was pregnant?"

"That's her, Arden Cade." Hugh clucked his tongue. "Poor kid. Being a single mom can't be easy under the best of circumstances, much less with gossips buzzing about the dad."

Garrett leaned forward on the couch. "Why? Who's the dad?"

"It's a big mystery. Far as anyone knew, she wasn't seeing anyone. Maybe it was a long-distance relationship with an out-of-town guy. People were shocked when she turned up pregnant and even more shocked those two brothers of hers didn't march the dude responsible into a shotgun wedding."

The fear he'd seen on Arden's face today flashed through his mind, and a completely insane thought struck him. *He* was an out-of-town guy. They'd used condoms, but those weren't effective one hundred percent of the time, were they? He'd heard stories.

"Out of…" His throat was so dry he had to try again. "Out of curiosity, do you know how far along she is?"

Hugh regarded him suspiciously but didn't challenge the bizarre question. "Hey, Darce? You have any idea how far along Arden is in her pregnancy?"

Darcy appeared in the doorway between rooms, drying her hands on a green-and-yellow-checkered towel. "Around six months, maybe? She said she's due the week of Thanksgiving."

Garrett's blood froze. *Six months.*

No, he was crazy to contemplate it. It was unfathomable that the woman who had been so open and expressive beneath him would keep a secret of this magnitude, cruelly excluding him. She knew he was friends with the Connors and could have found him easily. She could have called, emailed, sent a telegram—something! This was just his imagination running wild.

The unpleasant combination of newfound cynicism and sleepless nights had colored his judgment. The odds that Arden was pregnant by him… They'd used condoms, and they'd only been together one night.

Then again, Garrett himself was living proof that once was all it took.

"Layla, I am in trouble." Arden leaned back in the leather office chair, resenting the way it creaked. She hadn't gained *that* much weight. "Deep, deep trouble."

"Don't panic," her friend counseled over the phone. The words of wisdom were somewhat muffled around a bite of sandwich. In response to Arden's frantic text that morning, Layla was taking her lunch break in her car, away from the curious ears of students or fellow teachers.

"But he's here! Why is he here?"

"Um, didn't you say you met him because he was in town for a good friend's wedding? Makes sense that he'd occasionally visit said friend. The part I can't believe is that you saw him Sunday, yet waited until Tuesday to let me know."

"Because I spent yesterday in denial," Arden mumbled. She'd never been comfortable discussing her night with Garrett. It had felt so private, something meant only to be between them. Maybe if she'd known Layla back then, or if Natalie had still been alive… "Am I being punished for having a one-night stand? Am I a bad person?"

"Don't start pinning those scarlet *A*'s on your maternity clothes just yet. The fact that you'd only been with two men up until then is pretty solid evidence you're not a tramp."

"No, the fact that there had only been two previous lovers in my life is evidence that I have very large, very overprotective brothers," Arden said without rancor. Her brothers' local influence had probably helped prevent some impulsive mistakes in her teens. She nervously twisted the cord on the phone. "I think Justin suspects Garrett is the father. What if *Garrett* suspects as much?" So many emotions had rampaged through her when she'd seen him. She hadn't exactly maintained a poker face.

"Did he give you any reason to think that?"

"Not really. He was making small talk. I was busy freaking out."

"Then let's not borrow trouble," Layla advised. "Are you going to—"

"Oops, work beckons," Arden interrupted as the door to her studio swung open. "Maybe we can meet for dinner?"

"I don't know. I've got a stack of practice tests I have to grade so I can figure out how much my students forgot over the summer and plan accordingly. But give me a few hours to talk myself into it, and I'll text you later."

Arden disconnected, calling out, "Be with you in a second."

Over the summer, Layla had acted briefly as receptionist, but for the most part, Arden had always run a one-woman shop. She didn't get many random drop-ins. Customers usually called or emailed to schedule an appointment or, in the case of big events, to ask preliminary questions and do price comparisons.

Coming around the edge of her desk, she steadied herself with her hand. She was constantly readjusting to her ever-changing center of gravity.

"Hope I'm not interrupting your work." That smooth deep voice was exactly the same as it had been the first time he'd spoken to her, sending tremors through her body. Garrett Frost stood in the center of her reception area, cowboy hat in hand, an unreadable expression on his face.

Adrenaline surged, making her head swim. "Garrett." Her hands moved reflexively to cover the baby bump. That happened a lot lately when she was apprehensive.

He misinterpreted the protective gesture. "If you're trying to hide that you're expecting, it's a little late."

"I…I…" *Say something.* Preferably something intelligent. "Can I get you a cup of coffee?"

It wasn't until he shook his head that she realized she hadn't brewed any. She'd given it up during the pregnancy and hadn't been expecting clients for another few hours. Thank goodness he hadn't taken her up on the offer—her pride balked at the idea of making herself seem more ridiculous. She hadn't exactly been articulate at the grocery store.

"I'm sorry I was rude the other day," she said. "You took me by surprise. It was a shock, running in to you there."

"You weren't the only one stunned," he said pointedly. His gaze dropped before returning to her face.

"So, uh, how'd you find my office? Did your friend Hugh mention I was in this shopping center? I hope he and his wife are doing well." Her pulse was racing, and she heard her babbled words as though from a distance.

"Actually, I looked you up myself. Knowing your name and that you owned a photography studio was enough. It's not difficult to find someone, if you bother to look." His gray eyes were like thunderclouds. "If, for instance, a woman needed to locate a man, even one in a different town. I don't think there are many Garrett Frosts who are part owners of Colorado cattle ranches, but maybe I'm wrong. What do you think, Arden?"

She swallowed, knowing that his real question had nothing to do with addresses or phone books. He was asking if his suspicions were accurate, and she couldn't bring herself to answer. There was a huge difference between not tracking down a man to deliver life-altering news he probably didn't want to hear and actually lying to his face.

He took a step closer. "You seemed so startled to see me the other day. Terrified, as a matter of fact."

Feeling cornered, she took deep breaths, trying to lower her elevated blood pressure.

"Maybe I'm completely off base," he continued, "but extenuating circumstances have made me more distrustful than I used to be. If I'm wrong, you can laugh at me or indignantly cuss me out. But tell me the truth, Arden. Are you carrying my child?"

Chapter Four

Garrett had mentally rehearsed different ways this confrontation could play out—from her scoffing at his ludicrous accusation to her tearfully confessing all and begging his forgiveness. But he hadn't imagined her collapsing.

Her eyes rolled upward and she crumpled in on herself.

"Arden!"

He bolted toward her with just enough time to get his arms around her before she fell. What was he thinking, intimidating a pregnant woman? What if he'd caused harm to her or the baby? He lowered himself to the floor awkwardly, supporting her weight as he cradled her against his chest.

She blinked up at him, and it was such a relief to see those blue-green eyes open. At least she was conscious, although her chest rose and fell with alarmingly rapid exhalations. "G-Gar—"

"Shhh. Catch your breath first." He stroked her hair back from her pale face, feeling like an ogre. If he was right about the baby, then Arden owed him a major apology, but no matter how angry he was, he never would have deliberately hurt her.

She raised one shaky hand to press against her heart, her expression pained. "Water?"

He shrugged out of the lightweight denim jacket he'd been wearing, rolling it up as a makeshift pillow beneath her head. There was a water dispenser in the corner of the room, and he half filled a paper cup. "You have a history of fainting?" he asked. Maybe if this was something that happened routinely, he wouldn't feel like such a bastard.

"Only twice." She sipped her water, her words halting. "Overheated camping. Blacked out another time. When…I got bad news."

He wasn't sure whether this technically counted as fainting—had she lost consciousness completely? Was there a chance it would happen again when she was alone? "Should we get you to a doctor?"

She bit her lip, still struggling to breathe normally. "Probab— Probably overkill, but… The baby." Her eyes filled with tears, the palpable fear in her gaze knifing through him.

"Better safe than sorry." He helped her to her feet, noting her rocky balance.

"We have to lock up," she said. "Keys in my purse. Second desk drawer."

He got everything she asked for, then helped her out to the truck. She leaned against the seat, eyes closed. There was a lot they needed to say to each other, but it was challenge enough for her to give him rudimentary directions to the hospital.

The emergency room was fairly empty on a Tuesday afternoon. A mother sat in the far corner trying to coax a little girl to stop crying, and a burly man watched a daytime talk show with one eye while holding some kind of compress over the other. The blonde nurse working the admissions counter gasped softly when she spotted Garrett and Arden.

"Arden! You okay, hon?"

"Probably. I feel silly being here, but I think I fainted. Heart beating too fast, got dizzy…"

"Then you did the right thing by coming in." The blonde eyed Garrett with blatant curiosity but didn't ask who he was. "You two have a seat and fill out the forms on this clipboard. Oh, and this one for Obstetrics." She passed over a pale green sheet of paper.

Garrett caught sight of a long list of questions. None seemed as crucial as the one looming in his mind. *Who the hell is the father?*

"Need any help with those?" he offered.

"No!" Arden clutched the paperwork to her chest, not meeting his eyes. "I got it."

They sat down and she fumbled through her purse, retrieving her license and insurance card. Her hands were shaky as she muttered, "Damn, I hate hospitals."

He'd never thought much about them one way or the other. It occurred to him that Will Harlow could be in a hospital bed at this very moment, praying that his biological son agreed to give up a kidney.

Fury filled him, resentment at the secrets that had been kept. He struggled to keep his voice soft, non-threatening. "Arden, you owe me an answer." At least here, if she became overwrought by his questioning, there were medical professionals twenty feet away.

"I know." She turned to him, the tears shimmering in her apologetic gaze an unmistakable reply. Still, he couldn't quite force himself to accept the truth until she added out loud, "It's you. You're the baby's father."

Garrett hadn't thought he could ever be more shocked than when he'd learned about his mother and Will. He'd been wrong. *I'm a dad?* If he hadn't retreated to Cielo Peak to cope with the last bombshell a lying woman had dropped on him, he never would have known.

He clenched his fists against his thighs. "What were you planning to tell the kid? Children should know who their fathers are!"

The clipboard trembled in her grasp. "To be honest, I hadn't thought that far ahead. I was already a couple of months pregnant by the time I realized what had happened, and the discovery was mind-blowing. I needed time to adjust."

He knew the feeling. But he was too angry to sympathize.

"Garrett, I—"

"Someone from Obstetrics is on the way down with a wheelchair." The blonde admissions nurse walked toward them. "They'll get you in a real room instead of one of these E.R. cubicles, probably put you on a fetal monitor for an hour or so to make sure the baby's not in distress. Ask you some questions, maybe take some blood, check for anemia. You want me to contact either of your brothers, hon?"

"No! The last thing Colin needs is another phone call from a hospital E.R.," Arden said adamantly. "And I figure calling Justin would be awkward for you."

"You mean because he dumped me?" the woman asked with a wry smile. She seemed more amused than heartbroken. "Don't worry, I knew what I was getting into with that one. It was fun while it lasted. Talking to him won't upset me, I promise. Would you like him to be here?"

"Not unless I'm going to need the ride." Arden slid a questioning glance in Garrett's direction. "Are you planning to stick around?"

He folded his arms over his chest, smiling for the nurse's benefit. "You couldn't get rid of me if you tried, sweetheart."

ARDEN STUDIED THE ceiling intently, as if the answers to her problems might magically be found in the speckled tiles overhead. She'd gained a momentary reprieve when Garrett stepped out of the room so she could change, but he'd be knocking on the door any second. She hadn't missed his smirk when she'd asked for the privacy—after all, he'd already seen her naked. That was how they'd landed in this mess.

"Not that I think you're making a mess of my life," she whispered guiltily, as if the baby had heard her tormented thoughts. Arden was plenty grateful for her child. She was just second-guessing her decision to raise the child alone, Garrett none the wiser. *But I am alone.* She and Garrett had no real history or future. How was she going to share the most precious thing in her life with a man she barely knew?

Instead of knocking, Garrett cracked the door open a quarter of an inch, calling out before entering. "You decent in there?"

In a thin piece of fabric that tied behind her and left most of her back exposed? Hardly. "Close enough, I guess."

He strolled into the room, filling it with his size. Having grown up with brothers, she normally found the presence of a strong man comfortingly familiar. But now trepidation rippled through her. Her brothers had never been as furious with her as Garrett seemed.

She expected him to interrogate her about the baby, but he surprised her. "That nurse downstairs—" he began.

"Sonja."

"She asked about your brothers. Not your parents?"

Arden kneaded the hospital blanket that covered her lap. "They're both dead. My brothers are pretty much all I have."

"Two of them, right? Colin and Justin?" At her nod, he continued. "Is this why Justin looked like he wanted to put his fist through my face at the grocery store—because I got you pregnant?"

"I think…" She averted her gaze. "I'm not sure what he picked up on between us, but I think he suspects you're the dad. He couldn't know for sure, though. I never told anyone who the father was."

"No kidding." Despite his soft tone, the biting sarcasm in his voice made her flinch.

"Garrett, I'm sorry. I—"

"Don't!" This time, he wasn't soft-spoken at all. Even he looked taken aback by the vehement outburst. He cleared his throat. "I've heard that particular phrase far more than any man should in one week. Enough already."

She frowned. Someone besides her had reason to apologize to him? Whoever it was should feel grateful to Arden—it was doubtful anyone else's transgression topped hers.

Garrett paced the room. Although he might have regained verbal control, forcing himself to *sound* calm, he couldn't mask the tension radiating from his body. "So is there a specific reason you hate hospitals? You mentioned Colin and emergency rooms. Did—"

"Knock, knock!" The cheerful voice preceded a gray-haired doctor poking his head inside the room. "I'm Dr. Wallace. I hear we're having some dizziness and tachycardia today?"

Why did doctors speak in plural like that, Arden wondered, as if using the royal we? "Does *tachycardia* mean my heart tried to pound through my chest?" she asked wearily.

"It's when your heart beats abnormally fast, yes. There are several reasons it can happen during pregnancy." Dr. Wallace went over the possibilities while looking at the vitals the nurse had collected. Then he checked the baby's heartbeat. "Just a precaution, of course. We have no reason to think anything's wrong with the little guy. Or gal."

Arden had grown accustomed to the use of fetal dopplers in her OB appointments and the reassuring *whoosh-whoosh* sound, but she'd forgotten this was Garrett's first time. He went completely still, the restless anger that had been palpable a few minutes ago fading into wonderment. His eyes widened.

"That's the heartbeat?" he asked reverently. "It's fast."

"Well within the standard range," Dr. Wallace assured them. But as Nurse Sonja had predicted, the doctor wanted to monitor Arden and the baby for some readings before letting them leave the hospital. He pushed Arden's gown up farther, the preliminary gel a cool tickle against her skin.

Although the sheet on the hospital bed kept her lower half covered, embarrassment heated her face. The last time Garrett had seen her unclothed, she'd looked a lot different than she did now.

When she was younger, Arden had stayed in shape by trying to keep up with her two athletic brothers. She'd been trim most of her life, and grief after Natalie's and Danny's deaths had robbed her of her appetite. Since her pregnancy had begun to show, she'd often felt awkward, but never fat—a growing baby was a healthy one. At the moment, however, vanity reared its head. Would Garrett be repulsed by her swollen body?

Why should you care if he is? Their night together had been amazing, but it had also been a one-time occurrence. It wasn't as if she wanted him to find her attractive. Even if she did, she suspected not contacting him about the baby had forever tarnished her in Garrett's eyes.

Within moments, the doctor had the sensors in place. "You try to relax, young lady, and I'll be back to check on you later. Meanwhile, I'll have the nurse bring you some water. It's important to stay hydrated."

All too soon, he was gone, leaving her and Garrett alone once more.

"You want to have a seat?" she offered. It was a small room, and the only chair would put him in uncomfortably close proximity to her. Yet almost anything seemed preferable to his earlier pacing. His taut strides made her think of caged predators.

He sat, but kept shifting position, obviously ill-at-ease. "Have you, um, had other problems during the pregnancy? Everything okay with you and the baby?"

"The doctors say everything's normal, even my being sick as a dog well into the second trimester." But she worried sometimes. It was frustrating to wake up with a sharp pain at three in the morning and have no one she could talk to about her fears. Early on, she'd posted a question to an online forum for soon-to-be-mothers. Despite a couple of helpful responses, the possibility of misinformation and the discovery that some people were far too willing to share horror stories had kept her from doing so again. "Apparently nausea can be a good sign that the baby's nice and strong. Plus, my being too sick to run the office alone led to hiring Layla, and she became a good friend. I…needed a friend."

Did Garrett hear the ache in her voice, the echo of solitude that had plagued her for so many months? What he'd said down in the emergency room was true. She *did* owe him answers. Starting with the night they'd met.

"My brother Colin married my best friend several years ago," she said haltingly. "Natalie and I had been best friends since kindergarten, the year my mom died. Colin's a great guy, but he's always had too much responsibility. He rarely laughed. Natalie changed that. She changed him. He doted on her and their baby boy. But then Nat and Danny were killed in a car accident."

Garrett watched her silently, obviously unsure what to do with this information but not interrupting.

"It destroyed Colin and devastated me. The day your

friend Hugh got married? That was Natalie's birthday, the first one I didn't get to spend with her as far back as I could remember. I was in a lot of pain that day. Meeting you was about the best thing that could happen to me. You were…" She broke off, assailed by memories that seemed excruciatingly intimate with him sitting only inches from her side. He'd been by turns tender and passionate, driving her need to such a sharp peak that there'd been no room in her for any other emotion.

On sheer impulse, she reached over and squeezed his hand. "Thank you."

He looked taken aback. "Uh, my pleasure."

"Having a baby was the furthest thing from my mind," she added. "At first I was too shocked to be scared or happy. But I've been around death, too much of it, and the idea of bringing a new life into the world… This may sound insane to you, but it almost felt like a goodbye present from Natalie. Some sort of cosmic full circle."

"And there wasn't room in that circle for anyone else?" He abandoned his chair in favor of resumed pacing.

Six months ago, he'd helped heal her hurting. The last thing in the world she wanted was to wound him. Another apology hovered on the tip of her tongue, but she recalled his hostile reaction to her previous attempt.

"I hardly knew anything about you," she reminded him. "I tried to imagine how my brother Justin would react if he discovered, completely out of the blue, that a near stranger was carrying his child. It was daunting. By the time the nausea and confusion subsided, months had passed. You could have had a serious girlfriend, plans for the future I would be ruining! Telling you seemed like too big a risk. After a lot of sleepless nights, I decided it would be best for my child to have no father than one who might resent it."

He stopped his pacing and stared her down. "So you were protecting both me and the baby by keeping the news to yourself?" His chuckle was like broken glass. "I wonder if all mothers have this gift for rationalizing dishonesty."

All mothers?

The slight knock at the door made them both jump, and a nurse entered with a pitcher of ice water and some plastic-wrapped cups. She drew up short, her smile fading as she registered the tension in the room.

"I hope I'm not interrupting," she said hesitantly. "Dr. Wallace asked me to bring some water."

Garrett nodded his head at her, making a visible effort not to appear intimidating. "Much appreciated, ma'am."

The nurse smiled at him before asking Arden, "Is there anything else you need?"

Yeah, a do-over button. Or, barring that, the words that would make Garrett understand what she'd been feeling, her belief that she was making the right decision for all three of them. What were the odds that the hospital stocked second chances and forgiveness alongside the antibiotics and lime Jell-O?

AFTER HER RELEASE from the hospital, Arden had tried to talk Garrett into driving her back to her car. "You can follow me home if you're worried about me," she'd proposed. But he'd categorically refused. Now, as she struggled to keep her eyes open, she found herself grateful for his inflexibility. If anyone had asked her a few hours ago, she would have sworn the day's events had left her too shaken to sleep for a week. But one of the periodic side effects of pregnancy was a full-body fatigue so encompassing it bordered on paralysis.

By the time Garrett pulled his truck into her driveway, the September sun was dipping below the horizon.

"This is it." She smothered a yawn. "Home sweet home." In terms of square footage, the cozy two-bedroom house was actually smaller than her former apartment. But once she'd learned she was pregnant, she'd wanted to own something, a place that was all hers. *Mine and the baby's.*

Besides, while walking up three flights of stairs every day might have been one of the lifestyle choices that helped keep her in shape, it would be more difficult to navigate while carrying boxes of diapers and an infant car seat. She'd traded all those steps for a neatly fenced-in postage stamp of a yard. Did it look sad and despondent to a rancher who was used to the open range, hundreds of acres of pastureland where cattle grazed beneath the Colorado sky? Based on Garrett's grudgingly solicitous manner, from not leaving her side at the hospital to not letting her get behind the wheel, she wouldn't be surprised if he insisted on walking her inside. Would he judge the meager surroundings inadequate for his child?

"This is a really good school district," she blurted.

He quirked an eyebrow at the spontaneous announcement.

Her face warmed. "Just thinking ahead." By five

years, plus or minus. Even though she might not be living here when it came time for the baby to go to kindergarten, she was doing her best to make all the right decisions.

She slanted a glance at Garrett's stony profile. Ironically, she may have already botched her biggest parenting decision thus far.

As he helped her down from the truck, she couldn't help noting that his hand was warm and callused. How did a man with labor-roughened skin caress a woman with such silky gentleness? The way he'd touched her—*Whoa.* Where had that memory come from? She shook her head as if she could physically dislodge the mental image.

He frowned. "Everything okay? You look flushed."

"Pregnancy comes with a lot of weird side effects." Like hormones in hyperdrive. Mostly, those hormones had manifested themselves in very vivid, very detailed dreams that made her blush the next morning. One of the more anecdotal pregnancy books had mentioned the phenomenon, and the author advised women to enjoy the perk. But it was disquieting to experience that surge of lust in front of Garrett.

She yanked her hand out of his. When his expression grew even stormier, she tried to mitigate her action with a lame explanation. "I, ah, need to get my keys." As she unlocked the front door, her stomach emitted an embarrassing rumble. Hunger ran a close second to exhaustion.

"I'm starving," he commented. "Didn't get around to eating lunch today."

"Me neither."

"Let's get you situated and decide on a plan for food. Maybe I can whip up something for dinner."

"I don't know about that." She stepped inside, flashing a sheepish glance over her shoulder. "My grocery shopping got cut short the other day. The kitchen's not fully stocked."

Should she mention the nearby pizza place that delivered? Would she be able to sit through a meal in Garrett's presence, or would nerves keep her from eating? She appreciated how civil he was being, but the friction between them was as pointed as it had been when he strode into her office today. She was too drained to withstand much more.

Needing to get off her feet before she fell off them, she made a beeline for the ratty armchair she'd found at a rummage sale years ago. She'd had it steam-cleaned with the distant plan of someday reupholstering. Since she'd never gotten around to that part, the chair looked like blue-plaid hell, but it was inexplicably comfortable.

Garrett was slow to follow. After a moment, she realized he was examining the framed pictures on her wall.

"Did you take all of these?" he asked.

"Yes."

Portraits of Justin and Colin were scattered among a jumble of other subjects, from a black-and-white shot of a stone well to a close-up of a light purple dahlia bud in midbloom. There was a landscape photo taking up too much space; she'd squeezed it in to replace the family picture of Colin with his wife and son that had been exiled to temporary storage in her closet.

"You're very talented," Garrett said. "Darcy and

Hugh showed me their wedding album. They were thrilled with your work."

She swallowed, briefly closing her eyes. "Do they know about the baby?" Had Garrett told them about how she'd jumped into bed with him, shared his suspicions that this baby was his? Lord, what they must think of her. "I mean, of course they know I'm pregnant, I've seen them in town. But do they know…?"

"That I'm a daddy? How the hell could I have told them when *I* didn't even know?" he exploded. He began pacing, not that there was much more space here than he'd had in the hospital room. In a slightly calmer voice, he asked, "Does the idea of anyone knowing we were together bother you so much? I've never felt like a woman's dirty secret before."

"It's not like that," she said miserably. "It has nothing to do with you." She recalled the pitying looks her teachers had given her after her father died, the local news stories after Natalie's crash. She hated for anyone to have reason to talk about her and her family. But Garrett shouldn't be penalized for her hang-ups.

He rubbed his temple absently. "It's not as if your neighbors are gonna buy that the stork brought the baby. So who cares if they know it was me?"

"I'm handling this badly." She sighed. "I've never… I'm pretty inexperienced."

"You mean because you're a first-time mom?"

"Inexperienced with men. And, um, sex in general." At his startled look, she added, "I'd had sex before— just, infrequently. And only with long-term boyfriends I knew really, really well. I'm *not* ashamed of what happened between us. I'm just at a loss for... If I say 'I'm sorry' again, are you going to yell?"

His sudden grin was so unexpected and striking that it made her knees weak. *Thank God I'm already sitting.*

"No yelling," he promised.

"Thank you. I am sorry. I don't know what I'm doing." There were manuals and chat rooms, even documentary-style television shows that revolved around pregnancy and birth. But none of them had outlined the protocol for how to weather whispered rumors, or break the news to appalled, overprotective brothers or how to cope with the gorgeous one-night stand you'd never expected to see again.

His smile faded. "If you'd told me the truth, maybe we could have figured it out together. For the record, since you broached the subject today, there's no girlfriend, serious or otherwise."

The declaration warmed her far more than it should have. *Not because I'm interested in him romantically, but because I'd hate to complicate a third person's life with all of this.*

"Based on what Hugh said, can I safely assume there's no guy in the picture?" he asked.

She almost laughed at the suggestion that she was dating anyone. How many men fantasized about meeting a gal who barfed for months on end, then began steadily swelling to the size of a beluga? The hint of vulnerability that flickered in Garrett's gaze sobered her. Did he worry that someone else was poised to play the role of father to his child?

"No guy," she said softly. *Except you.*

His tense shoulders lowered the merest fraction of

an inch. There was relief and something less definable in his eyes. Possessiveness? Awareness sizzled through Arden, replacing her earlier lethargy with something more energetic. And far more complicated. Her voice caught in her throat.

Changing the subject, he clapped his palms together. "Point me in the direction of the kitchen. I'll check out the dinner options."

"I wasn't kidding about rations being low." She used the arms of the chair to hoist herself upward. "But I think we can manage salad and some grilled cheese sandwiches."

As someone who lived alone, she wasn't used to anyone else puttering around in her kitchen. Letting him wait on her would just be too weird. "Can I offer you something to drink? I don't have any sodas or beer, but there's lemonade or filtered water. I could brew some tea."

"Lemonade sounds great." He trailed her into the kitchen.

"I'll get glasses. Lemonade's in the fridge," she directed. "And there should be some fruit salad left."

He turned to the refrigerator but stopped when he caught sight of the sonogram photos secured with promotional magnets from the Donnelly ski lodge. The first picture was from so early in the pregnancy that the baby was a mere peanut-shaped blip; a circle the doctor had drawn in ink showed where the heart was. But the other pictures were from a recent appointment. It was easy to make out the baby's head and profile.

"So, um, that's the little guy. Figuratively speaking," she clarified. "I have no idea what the gender is. I've decided to be surprised." She'd had trouble explaining her decision to friends and family, but there had been enough ugly surprises in Arden's life. Why not revel in one that was wonderful? "I've been calling the baby Peanut since I'm not sure what pronoun to use."

Garrett traced his thumb lightly over the edge of a photo. "These are amazing. To have such a clear look at someone who's not even... I've looked at bovine sonograms, but this—"

"Did you just compare pictures of our unborn child to those of *cows?*" she interrupted with mock indignation. Reaching around him, she pulled butter and cheese from the refrigerator.

He shrugged. "Hey, it's the life I know. Sleep with a cowboy, you gotta expect the occasional livestock mention."

"Good to know. I'll keep that..." *In mind for next time.* The thoughtless words evaporated from her lips. Next time? With whom? Certainly not him.

For starters, her major lie of omission probably guaranteed there would never be anything tender between her and Garrett. That aside, romance of any kind had dropped completely off her list of priorities for the time being. She hoped that, eventually, she and Garrett could overcome the strain between them for their child's sake, and develop a smooth, cordial relationship. Romantic entanglement was a risk that didn't make sense. Long-distance dating was difficult under the best of circumstances, and if they braved a relationship, only to have it end badly... *I'll take 'Ways to Make an Awkward Situation Even Worse' for a thousand, Alex.*

No, definitely not worth the gamble.

Casting about for a neutral topic, she placed buttered bread in the skillet. Since he'd made the joke about livestock, she decided that maybe his ranch was the safest subject.

"When you first told me what you do for a living," she began, "you sounded like you really love it. Do you think you would have eventually found your way into ranching even if you hadn't grown up surrounded by cattle and horses?"

He leaned against the kitchen counter, considering the question. "I honestly can't say. It's so much a part of who I am that I never gave any thought to another line of work. If I had to be cooped up inside an office like Hugh every day, I'd go stark raving mad. Running the Double F alongside my father… He's a hell of a man. I always wanted to be—" He broke off, his jaw clenched. Tension lined his rugged face.

Was there conflict between Garrett and his dad? Arden flipped the cheese sandwiches, backtracking quickly. "What about your mom?" Her voice was too shrill with forced cheer, and she struggled to sound natural. "Are the two of you close?"

"Not currently." He set the bowls of fruit salad on the table with a muted crash.

Strike two. "Any, uh, brothers? Sisters?"

"Only child."

She chuckled bleakly. "You with no siblings, me with no parents. It's like, between the two of us, we have enough puzzle pieces to make a whole family."

"A family." His expression darkened. "Maybe under different circumstances, we could have been. Maybe I would've known what it was like to teach my own son how to ride a horse, how to drive a tractor." He stared her down, so much pain in his steely gaze that it stopped her breath. "You know what? I'm not hungry, after all. Guess I'll head back into town."

Garrett, wait. At least eat something before you leave. She followed him, but her protests never made it any farther than her mind. She'd made a sufficiently disastrous mess of things for one night. Given his charged mood and her own emotional unpredictability, it was probably best to let him go.

He hesitated at the door, his look almost menacing. "I'll be in touch soon. Like it or not, we have a lot to discuss. I won't be a stranger in my child's life, Arden." With that, he left.

Possibly to do online research on Colorado family law and paternity rights. He'd looked furious. Was he enraged enough to challenge her for custody?

She pushed the horrible thought away. Garrett was a good man. Yes, she'd screwed up by not telling him of her own volition that he would be a father, but the baby wouldn't be here for another few months. She prayed that was enough time to somehow make this right.

Chapter Five

Garrett pulled over at the end of Arden's street and texted Hugh, asking if his friend could meet him in town. Fifteen minutes later, both men were parking their vehicles outside Hugh's favorite bar. The place didn't look like much—the lot was gravel rather than pavement and a couple of the light poles had burned-out bulbs—but Garrett had been here before and knew that the food was good and the drinks were reasonably priced.

"Thanks for joining me," Garrett said, his words brusque but sincere. "Feels like I've been asking you for a lot of favors lately. Hope I didn't interrupt you and Darcy's dinner."

"Nah, she's got book club at a friend's and isn't even home. For tonight, it's just us guys." Hugh squinted at him in the dim lighting. "So this might be a good time to finally tell me what brings you to town. Besides my obvious awesomeness."

Garrett had no idea where to begin. The astonishment over his mother's confession was still fresh, but now there was the tangle of Arden's deception, too. He felt battered by lies and weighty decisions he needed to make. "What would you do if Darcy ever lied to you?"

"What, you mean like about how expensive a pair of boots were?" Hugh asked.

"No. About something major."

Shaking his head, Hugh reached for the door to the bar. "She wouldn't do that."

Isn't that what Garrett had told himself twenty-four hours ago? That Arden Cade wasn't the kind of person who would hide her pregnancy from the baby's father? Lord, had he been wrong. But maybe he shouldn't be surprised. Apparently the closeness he'd felt between them during their night together had been merely superficial. An illusion. What did he really know about her?

That she's a talented photographer and a young woman who's lost too many people in her life, that she's scared but already loves this baby fiercely. He didn't want to empathize with her, but he couldn't help admiring how she'd dealt with the deaths of her best friend, her nephew and her parents. Even though he was avoiding his own mother right now, the thought of either of his folks dying one day turned his stomach and made his flesh clammy.

The men stepped inside and waited for the hostess to find them an available booth.

Amid the bar's many neon lights, the concern on Hugh's face was unmistakable. "I don't want to push, but, buddy, you look like you're gonna snap if you don't talk to someone."

It was a fair assessment. "Okay, but this conversation will require some time. And definitely some beer."

"CANNOT BELIEVE YOU'RE gonna be a daddy," Hugh slurred. It wasn't the first time he'd made the declaration. "I assumed it would be me before you. Since I'm, you know, actually married."

"Hey, I figured it would be you and Darcy first, too." Accepting reality was a cyclical process, one he'd been stuck repeating all day. It was like trying to unknot gnarled fishing line—each time he thought he was making progress, he'd have to start all over again.

"Have another glass," Hugh suggested sympathetically. He'd gone through more than half the pitcher while Garrett, now the designated driver, was busy spilling the story. Or at least an abbreviated version of it. He got through the upsetting news of his mom's affair, which had spawned this trip, to the secret of Arden's pregnancy. But he left aside the issue of Will needing a kidney transplant for now. It was too much for one night.

Garrett shook his head. "I don't think a second beer is really a long-term solution." Considering how Justin Cade had glowered at him the other day, maybe Arden's brothers would ultimately drop him off a steep cliff and eliminate the need for long-term plans. "Look, about Arden...I don't think she's really eager for people to know who the father is. The details—"

"Are her business. And yours," Hugh said firmly. "I won't keep secrets from my wife, but don't worry. Darcy and I won't spread any gossip."

"Y'all are the best," Garrett said, genuinely grateful. For the first time in days, he felt as if he could count on someone. Life had thrown him nothing but curveballs lately, and it was nice to be reminded that he had people in his corner. Hugh was as good a friend now as he'd always been in the past.

Garrett found himself nostalgic for the much simpler past. The present was full of perplexing psychological land mines. And he had no idea what to do about the future.

WHILE ARDEN UNLOCKED her studio early Wednesday morning, Justin impatiently shifted his weight behind her.

"Your secrecy is freaking me out," he complained. "First you were cagey about why you needed me to drive you to work this morning, now you won't tell me why you've called a family meeting."

The three siblings had long ago agreed that Cade family meetings were never to be called lightly and that attendance was mandatory.

Arden shot him a quelling look. "Of course I'll tell you—when the other part of the family gets here."

Justin went straight for the coffee supplies in the corner and began filling the pot with water. "You had a 'dizzy spell' yesterday and a friend drove you home," he commented. "Which friend? If it was Layla, you would've said so. I know there's something you're leaving out. You were a lousy liar as a kid, and you haven't improved with age."

She stood next to the coatrack, shrugging out of her jacket. "I got dizzy enough that I went to the hospital, okay? But I don't want Colin to know, so you'd better not mention it. He does *not* need any extra reason to worry that something will happen to me or the baby."

Justin was quick to agree. "My lips are sealed. Look, I'm as concerned about him going round the bend as you are. But you can tell *me* this stuff, okay? I'm too shallow to stay up nights obsessing over other people's safety."

The big faker. "No, you're not." The women he jilted might think of him as a heartless beast, but Arden knew there was more to him than that. Why was he so reluctant to let people see his caring side? "You've been a fantastic brother these past few months, and I don't know how I would have coped without you."

"Ah, is that what the family meeting's about?" he asked, spinning around a low-backed chair and straddling it. "Am I getting a medal for outstanding brothership? Is there a cash award involved? Because there's this new girl who works at the deli across from the ambulance station, and I would love to take her out for a night on the town."

Ignoring him, she booted up her computer for the day. Given Justin's flippant personality, he might be kidding about the girl at the deli. But if he was serious, she'd rather not know. His hit-and-run dating habits were too exasperating. She'd never seen him happier than he'd been with Elisabeth Donnelly. She understood that Elisabeth's life had changed drastically after being named guardian of a little girl, but she believed Justin had made a grave mistake walking away from the woman he loved. A gust of wind swept through the studio when the front door opened again, and her heart jumped to her throat. *Colin.* While she'd decided that this conversation with her brothers was necessary, she dreaded having to go through with it. Silly, really. Wasn't the hardest part telling them she was pregnant in the first place? Relatively speaking, explaining who the father was should be a piece of cake.

She watched her brothers exchange greetings. Colin's hello was terse, his voice a low rasp. He had his motorcycle helmet tucked under one arm, and his rich brown hair had grown shaggy, falling across his forehead. It almost covered his turquoise eyes, which resembled hard stone in more than just color. All in all, not someone you'd want to encounter in a dark alley.

It tugged at her heart that he tried, for her benefit, to smile. Even if it was a dismal failure. "Morning, Colin."

"You…look good. Glowing and all that."

"Thank you." She hugged him, trying not to be offended by how he stiffened at her embrace. The man who'd once cuddled her after nightmares and skinned knees could no longer bear to be touched.

He patted her on the back, then stepped away. "You haven't called a family meeting since you told us you were expecting. What's wrong?"

She heaved a sigh. "Didn't I say in the message, like ten times, that everything was okay and not to worry? That I just needed to talk to you guys?"

"Maybe this is when she tells us she's having twins," Justin mused.

"No." She led them to the table where she normally showed clients their photo selections, and they all took a seat. "This is when I tell you about the baby's father."

"About damn time." The playfulness vanished from Justin's gaze. "Tell me you've talked to him and that he's taking responsibility for what he did."

"What *he* did?" She rolled her eyes. "Where do you think I was in all this?"

Colin held up a hand, looking pale. "No details!"

She interlocked her fingers, trying not to fidget while

she searched for the right words. "I told you that you guys didn't know him—"

"Which I've always found suspect," Justin interjected. "We know pretty much everyone you know."

"Well, I didn't know him, either," she admitted. "He was an out-of-town guest at a wedding I shot. I'd only met him that night."

"You went to bed with a total stranger?" Colin roared. "And didn't have safe sex?"

Her face flamed, but she didn't get the chance to explain that they'd used protection.

"Do you have any idea how dangerous that was?" Justin demanded.

"Hey." She slammed her palms down on the table. "*No* yelling at the pregnant lady. It's not good for me or Peanut. We were careful. Or tried to be." She wagged her finger at Justin. "And you don't get to comment on my love life, you hypocrite. How many women have you slept with whose last names you didn't even know?"

He ground his teeth but didn't argue.

"I needed that night. It was Natalie's birthday, and I just—" She broke off, assessing her oldest brother. There was a time when his late wife's name made him flinch. Now he stared woodenly ahead. Difficult to tell whether that was progress.

She swallowed hard, picking up the thread of her story. "The next day, Garrett left town and went back to his regularly scheduled life. I was stunned to learn I was pregnant, but I saw it as a gift. Almost like…Natalie's gift to me. I didn't see him as part of the equation. Until he came to town for an unexpected visit."

"The guy from the grocery store!" Justin declared. "It's him, isn't it?"

She nodded. "He deduced that the baby is his, and he's justifiably *irritated*." The emphasis she put on the word kept it from being a laughable understatement.

Colin's scowl deepened. "What did he say? If he thinks he's going to upset *my* sister, I—"

"I do search and rescue," Justin said. "I know plenty of obscure places where no one would find his body."

"And you two boneheads don't understand why I wouldn't tell you who he was? Garrett isn't the one who messed up. He thought he was taking a few days in Cielo Peak for rest and relaxation, he wasn't expecting his life to get turned upside down. The thing is, I'm not sure how long he's staying and I need to…fix this. I don't want him hating me. Or suing me for custody. Or—"

"He threatened to take your baby?" Colin's voice was raw murder.

"No! That's an over-the-top, sleep-deprived worst-case scenario." The most recent of her 2:00 a.m. panic attacks, which ranged from concerns about genetic predispositions to wondering how difficult it would be to master the art of nursing. "Justin, if you're not on call tonight, I want to invite Garrett to dinner so you two can meet him."

"Absolutely," Justin said with relish. He and Colin exchanged bloodthirsty glances that detonated Arden's temper. A tsunami of conflicting emotions and pregnancy hormones crashed over her.

"Enough with the insane big-brother crap!" she thundered. "I don't need someone's knees broken. I need *support.* Mom's not here to hold my hand, to soothe my panic when I suddenly can't remember how long it's been since I felt the baby move. Nat was my best friend in the world, and she would've been supportive without judging me, but she's gone, too. After Thanksgiving, something between the size of a five-pound and ten-pound bag of potatoes is going to come *out of my body,* and then starts the *really* difficult stuff! I have to figure out how to raise a kid alone. Do I make enough money as a photographer? Even with Layla's generous offers of weekend and summer babysitting, how will I be able to take as many jobs? I've been terrified of screwing up, yet it seems like I already have. I kept Garrett in the dark, and I have no one but myself to blame if he detests me. One family dinner isn't going to make things right, but it's a start. You two are going to help me. You will come to my house for dinner, and *you will be nice!* Got it?"

Belatedly, Arden realized she was breathing hard. And standing. When had she shot out of her chair?

"Damn." Justin turned to Colin, lowering his voice to a stage whisper. "So much for *you* being the scariest Cade."

As someone who loved being outdoors, Garrett should be having more fun. The scenery was breathtaking, and the crisp bite to the early autumn air was a refreshing counterpoint to the bright sunshine. He knew Darcy had suggested this midmorning hike to keep him entertained while Hugh was at work, but Garrett spent a lot of hours with stoic ranch hands and equally nonverbal cows. He was unprepared for Darcy's nonstop, effervescent commentary.

"Don't you worry," Darcy had chirped on their drive to the trail's entrance. "Hugh told me everything, and I won't pester you with questions about you-know-who. We're going to get your mind off your problems!"

Evidently, her treatment for a troubled mind included two steps: fresh air and more information on birds than any normal human being could process in a lifetime. The summer day he'd first met Darcy, he'd commented on the finch tattoo across her shoulder blade and learned she loved birds. But he'd never known until now how much ornithological detail she could pack into a discussion.

Although, weren't discussions multisided? This fell more into the category of an academic lecture. Somehow, she'd worked her way around to the topic of orioles and their intricate nests, which she called "engineering marvels."

"They're really quite spectacular," she continued happily.

Garrett hoped his eyes didn't glaze over, or he might end up aimlessly walking off the mountain. He made a nominal effort to listen, but he was busy imagining an oriole hatchling hit with the news that his father was some other bird. *Actually, son, you know that cardinal a couple of trees over? I was going to tell you when you were old enough....*

The shock of Arden's pregnancy had temporarily eclipsed the reason Garrett had escaped to Cielo Peak in the first place. But now thoughts of Will Harlow were bubbling to the surface. Earlier, after navigating a particularly steep part of the trail, Darcy had become winded and asked to pause for water and a chance to catch her breath. She'd remarked that ranch work obviously kept Garrett in tip-top shape.

Garrett was beginning to realize that he often took his health for granted. He could climb mountains, gallop across a pasture on horseback or go for a spur-of-the-moment jog. *Or have really athletic sex with a woman you met at your friend's wedding reception.* Meanwhile, there was a man potentially dying whom Garrett might be able to save.

The funny thing was, if his mother had simply told him their old friend Will needed a kidney, Garrett probably would have agreed to be tested for compatibility. His driver's license already had him listed as a willing organ donor. But the way she'd gone about it… What would Garrett tell his dad? How long would recovery from surgery prevent working on the ranch?

It would be easier for Garrett if his dad knew the truth, if Brandon could give his understanding and approval of the decision.

"Oh! Warbler." Darcy's voice was a delighted whisper. She abandoned what she'd been saying and made her way up the path, reaching for her binoculars as she went. Garrett stayed where he was, drinking in the silence.

A few minutes later, she returned, holding her cell phone out toward him. "You should see these shots I—" The phone began playing an obnoxiously catchy pop song Garrett dreaded having stuck in his head for the rest of the day.

"Hello?" Darcy answered. Her eyes widened. "Arden!

This is a pleasant surprise. His number? I can do better than that. He's standing right here. Garrett, it's for you."

Knowing who it was ahead of time didn't stop him from experiencing an electric jolt at the sound of her voice.

"I'm so glad I caught you." Arden's tone was husky. With nerves, or something else? "I didn't have your cell number, so I thought maybe your friends could help me track you down. I hope you don't mind?"

Aware that Darcy was watching with avid curiosity, he bit back the retort that the only thing he minded was Arden *not* tracking him down months ago.

"No, I'm glad you called. Has, um, something else happened?" She'd seemed completely stable when he'd left her house last night, but what did he know about pregnancy?

"With the baby, you mean? We're both fine," she assured him. "It's just… I was up all night thinking. About us."

His heart did an odd somersault in his chest. It was uncomfortable yet not entirely unpleasant.

"Like you said, we have to decide how this is going to work," she said, "how involved you'll be. For better or worse, we're a part of each other's futures. I think we owe it to ourselves to get to know each other."

His undisciplined thoughts strayed to how intimately he knew her. Clearing his throat, he turned away from Darcy. "Sounds reasonable."

"I'd like you to meet my brothers," she added shyly. "They're a big part of my life."

That half of the proposition sounded a lot less appealing than the first part. "If I have to."

He could hear the grin in her voice. "They're not that bad. Once you get used to them. I know it's short notice, but do you already have dinner plans?"

"Nothing concrete." The Connors would understand his absence—and could point the police in the right direction if the Cade menfolk helped him disappear.

"Then how about my house, seven o'clock?"

"I'll be there." He disconnected, thinking how bizarre it was that, without having been on a single date, he and Arden had progressed to the meeting-the-family phase. But then, he supposed that wasn't as unusual as getting a woman pregnant without ever having dated.

"THAT IS NOT LASAGNA!" Arden slammed the oven door in frustration.

"It isn't?" Layla asked hesitantly.

"No, that is soup. I've made freaking lasagna soup." Arden covered her eyes with her hands and battled the urge to cry. Or swear. Or break plates. Any of the three might make her feel better, but none seemed like a productive use of her time with guests arriving in less than an hour.

"It smells wonderful," Layla assured her, coming closer to inspect the pan through the oven window.

"Thanks. But I screwed up. Normally I buy oven-ready lasagna noodles. You don't have to boil them first." Arden's words grew more rapid as she recounted her mistake. "You just add some water to the pan before baking, but the store was out of my preferred kind and I had to get regular noodles, only I was distracted so I added extra water even though I didn't need it, and it doesn't look as if the extra liquid is absorbing so now—"

"Breathe!" Layla gently squeezed Arden's shoulder. "In case you haven't heard, four out of five doctors are now saying oxygen is important."

Arden rolled her eyes, momentarily abandoning the pasta diatribe. "Oh, good. Make jokes."

The petite redhead grinned. "Well, it seemed like a better way to fix your hysteria than slapping you." She took a peek at the lasagna. "That's not too bad. Worst-case scenario, your sauce is slightly runnier than usual, but I bet it'll still taste great. You know your brothers will eat anything you serve them."

True. They'd been her test subjects in the early years, when she'd first been learning to cook. But Garrett...

"I wanted to impress him," she admitted. "At first, I looked up fancy recipes online, but that felt pretentious. I also considered a steak dinner, which I rejected because it seemed too on-the-nose for a cattle rancher." And those were only the food deliberations. She didn't want to admit how much thought she'd put into her appearance. After changing three times, she'd settled on a silky, oversize deep purple blouse with a pair of stretchy black leggings—her feminine pride had balked at pants with built-in maternity panels. Thankful that pregnancy was making her hair so full and shiny, she'd pulled it into a high ponytail.

"Honestly," Layla said, "I doubt Garrett will pay much attention to the food, not with everything else you've given him to think about. You yourself hardly ate for months, until the surprise wore off."

"You're confusing surprise with nausea. I couldn't

hold down a damn thing." But she understood her friend's point. No matter what she served, one dinner would not magically solve the problems she and Garrett faced. "Did I remember to thank you for stopping by? You're a lifesaver."

Layla had brought a loaf of fresh bread from the bakery to go with the lasagna and salad. She'd also lent a hand with setting the table and chopping vegetables, doing her cheerful best to keep Arden calm. A tall order, since the two brothers who'd never fully approved of any man in her life were about to meet the stranger who'd fathered her baby.

"I don't suppose you want to stay for dinner?" Arden asked a bit desperately.

"Can't. I have a PTA thing, remember? But I will call and check on you tonight. Partly because I care and partly because your life is way more engrossing than mine." An only child, Layla was always fascinated by stories of Arden's brothers. Now that Garrett had been added to the mix, Layla said talking to Arden was better than watching television.

They both stiffened when the doorbell rang. Arden glanced at the digital clock over the stove. "It's not even close to time! None of them should be here yet."

"Relax," Layla advised. "For all you know, it's the mailman dropping off a package."

But when Arden followed her friend to the foyer, they saw Garrett through the wedges of decorative glass that framed the front door. He was striking in head-to-toe black that started with his cowboy hat and stopped with his boots.

"Whoa," Layla whispered, her hushed voice filled with awe. "Is that him?"

"Yep."

"A man that virile can probably get a girl pregnant just by smiling at her. You didn't stand a chance."

Arden opened the door, trying to look welcoming instead of exasperated by his untimely arrival. "H-hi."

"I'm early," he said without preamble. "I thought maybe I could help. And that if I arrived before your brothers, I'd be less likely to walk into some kind of ambush."

Layla laughed, and Arden shot her a look.

"This is my friend, Layla Green. She dropped by to assist, too. Great minds thinking alike and all that." She moved out of the way, allowing Garrett to step inside and shake Layla's hand.

"Nice to meet you, ma'am."

Ever since Arden had seen him at the supermarket, she'd been assailed by trepidation, viewing him through the eyes of a woman with reason to avoid him. But seeing him now, through Layla's openly appreciative gaze, she remembered how she'd felt that first night, how drawn she'd been to the handsome wedding guest with his slow, beckoning grin and silvery eyes that made all kinds of mysterious promises. In his hotel room with her that night, he'd fulfilled every one of those unspoken promises.

Heat suffused Arden. Her body had been so hypersensitive lately that the idea of him touching her skin now—

"Arden?" Garrett's voice was strangled.

"Y-yes?" She guiltily met his gaze, wondering if her thoughts had been clear on her face for everyone to see.

"I should be going," Layla said brightly. "You kids… have fun." Her car keys jingled as she pulled them from her cardigan pocket, and she scampered out of the house.

Come back, Arden wanted to call after her. *Save me from myself.*

Garrett reached over and pushed the front door shut without ever taking his eyes off her, then slowly advanced toward her. With the wall at her back, she had nowhere to go. Not that she had the willpower to make an escape, anyway. "You have to promise me something, Arden."

Anything.

"Do *not* look at me like that in front of your brothers. They'll have me run out of town before dessert."

"I, ah…" She wished she could feign confusion. It was so undignified to be caught mentally undressing him. "Sorry. Pregnancy hormones are— Words fail me."

Seeming intrigued by her explanation, he raised his hand, brushing the back of his knuckles over her jaw. "You think it's because of the pregnancy?"

"Yes." That and his return to Cielo Peak. "S-something to do with increased blood flow. The books say it's perfectly normal." Like swollen hands. Or heartburn. But she couldn't find her voice to mention those less charged symptoms.

"I haven't been able to get you out of my head all day," he said hoarsely. "Maybe that's the real reason I'm here early. After you called this morning, I started with platonic intentions, trying to think about what happens once the baby comes. But the longer my thoughts lingered on you, the more I couldn't help remembering…"

Her lips parted. Oh, God. Was he going to kiss her?

If he didn't, did she possess the self-discipline *not* to kiss him?

Somewhere in the furthest reaches of her desire-fogged brain, a small voice reminded her that her brothers would be here eventually. The last thing she wanted was for them to walk into her house and catch her seducing Garrett.

She held up both her hands, theoretically to ward him off, but when her palms met the hard wall of his chest, need spiraled through her. "We can't do this now."

"Now?" His eyebrows rose, and he grinned down at her.

"Er…it's probably not a great idea for later, either, but— Can I get you a drink? I could use some ice water. You heard what Dr. Wallace said about staying hydrated." She tried to duck away nonchalantly, putting a safe distance between them, but given the current proportions of her body, it was difficult to move casually. She waddled toward the kitchen, suddenly neurotic about what she looked like from behind.

"Whatever's cooking smells delicious," he said.

"Fingers crossed. I'm, uh, not sure the sauce is going to be the consistency I wanted. Guess we can always order take-out," she joked wanly.

"After you, the woman carrying my child, slaved over a home-cooked meal? No, ma'am. I don't care what comes out of that oven, we're eating it. My momma raised me better…" His expression, which had matched the protective warmth in his voice, grew shuttered as he trailed off.

She recalled when she'd asked him the other day if he and his mother were close. He'd said "not currently." Were they fighting? Estranged? A pang of melancholy stabbed her. She hoped he didn't let some argument or difference of opinion deprive him of a relationship with his mother. Life was short.

"Garrett, this may be out of line, but—*oomf.*" She pressed a hand to her midsection, where her unborn child had taken up soccer. Or was possibly auditioning for the Rockettes.

"You okay?" Garrett was at her side in a heartbeat.

"Fine. The baby's just kicking."

How was it possible to look ecstatic and apprehensive at the same time? His gray eyes flickered with both emotions. "Can I… Would you mind if—"

Instead of waiting for him to finish floundering through the request, she took his hand and settled it over her tummy. Another dramatic jab occurred, and while the high-kick routine being performed among her internal organs wasn't exactly comfortable, she was glad the movements were forceful enough for Garrett to feel them.

He gazed at her with such reverence it was humbling. "We really did make a baby." He said it like a blessing rather than an accident, and she felt closer to him in that instant than she ever had to anyone else.

Her eyes welled. "We really did."

He grazed the side of her face with his thumb, wiping away a tear. Then he bent and kissed the spot.

"Garrett." It was a plea, and they both knew it. She

was already stretching up to meet him, anticipation sizzling through her veins. She inhaled his clean masculine scent, which triggered a cascade of sense memories from their night together. It had been six and a half months since this man had kissed her. If she had to wait another six and a half seconds, she'd spontaneously combust. His lips brushed over hers, barely making contact, more tease than touch, and a small sound of need escaped her. Then he kissed her for real, taking possession of her mouth.

Sensation shot through her, igniting every nerve ending in her body. Her skin tingled, her breasts ached, her nipples tightened. She met his tongue with her own, gripping his shoulder with one hand and plunging the other through his hair. She was dimly aware of his hat hitting the floor. He tightened his hold on her hips, tugging her closer. While her shape made it difficult for them to be as perfectly aligned as she would have liked, he was near enough for her to feel his erection. She moaned, shifting restlessly in her attempts to nestle against him.

Abruptly, Garrett straightened, his breathing ragged. "I heard a car door."

No, no, no. *Not now!* She could barely form a coherent thought.

He leaned down and bit her bottom lip. "Rain check, sweetheart."

She was still leaning against the wall trying to catch her breath when the front door opened. Justin called out, "Hey, sis. I see we already have company?"

In addition to putting his hat back on, Garrett had grabbed a dishtowel and a bowl from the rack next to the sink, making it look as if he'd been helping in the kitchen rather than ravishing her. Holding the towel casually in front of him, he extended his free hand. "We didn't formally meet the other day. I'm Garrett Frost."

Her brother hesitated, and Arden cleared her throat to remind him of his promise to behave. "Justin Cade." He turned to her. "I wasn't expecting anyone else to be here yet. Thought I'd show up a few minutes early and see if you needed any help."

"Garrett and Layla both had the same idea—you just missed her," Arden added innocently, as if she and Garrett had been chaperoned rather than making out in her kitchen.

"Well, I can take over where she left off. You don't need to be on your feet."

She knew from a lifetime of experience that arguing never stopped either of her brothers from fussing over her. "I'll sit, but get the lasagna out of the oven for me, okay? It's got enough problems without the edges burning."

"Problems?" Justin scoffed. "Your lasagna is kick-ass." He shot Garrett a suspicious glance, as if the cowboy were to blame for Arden's uncharacteristic lack of culinary confidence. Both men reached to pull a chair out for her at the same time, nearly colliding. Justin took a step back, his expression mulish. "Hell, Arden, you could drop it on the floor first, and I'd still eat it."

Was that supposed to be flattering?

Garrett squared his shoulders, rising to the challenge. "Same here. I already told her we'd be eating anything she served, no matter how bad it is."

Arden smacked her forehead with her palm. She'd

expected some blatant displays of testosterone tonight, but she wished they'd leave her food out of it. Nonetheless, she knew how tough her brothers could be on other males in her life, so she offered Garrett an encouraging smile. He responded with a wicked grin that made her think he was mentally replaying their kiss. She blushed, earning a frown from her brother. Justin stepped between them to place salad dressing on the table, jostling Garrett in the process.

Why had she thought this dinner would be a good idea?

In an attempt to keep the men occupied with something other than sizing each other up, she almost asked for a volunteer to slice the bread. Then she decided she didn't want either alpha male holding a knife until they'd decided to play nice. When she heard Colin's motorcycle roar into the driveway, she barely stifled a groan. *Oh, goody. Because he excels at lightening the mood.*

This should go well.

Chapter Six

Garrett had immediately recognized that Justin Cade didn't like him. Yet, compared to Colin, Justin was a welcoming ray of sunshine. Colin didn't even smile when he greeted his sister. He squeezed her shoulder in what was probably meant as an affectionate gesture, his aquamarine eyes scanning her face intently as if convincing himself she was well.

Then he turned his head toward Garrett, his voice wintry. "You must be the father."

The wrong one of us is named Frost.

"We've heard about you," Colin added, his expression just shy of a sneer.

Garrett would have bristled at the cold animosity if Arden hadn't told him about her brother's tragic past. Was it difficult for Colin, who'd lost his own child, to be around a man who'd so casually, inadvertently, stumbled into fatherhood? "I'm Garrett. Arden's told me a lot about you, too."

She smiled, her expression a little desperate. "Now that we're all here, we should eat! Hope everyone's good and hungry. I know I am!"

From the way Justin raised his eyebrows, Garrett guessed Arden wasn't typically this high-strung. "My sister's nervous." Justin leveled the words at Garrett like an accusation, holding him responsible for Arden's increased stress. Considering that Garrett's conversation with her yesterday had landed her in the hospital, perhaps Justin had a point.

"Not at all," Arden denied. "I'm not nervous, I'm starving. You know, eating for two now."

"You have any sisters, Frost?" Justin asked.

Garrett shook his head. "Only child." This information was met with a curled lip, as if not having siblings was a personal failing or meant he didn't value family. "My parents and I are very close." Except, of course, that his dad wasn't actually his father but didn't know it. And Garrett wasn't technically speaking to his mom.

Other than that, they were a tightly knit unit.

Arden shepherded everyone to the table. Her brothers sat at the two ends, and Garrett found himself with the best view in the house—directly across from Arden. He couldn't recall ever seeing anyone who blushed as easily as she did. Was it that increased blood flow she'd mentioned? Whatever the reason, her rosy cheeks made her look as if she'd just come in from the cold. Which made him want to cuddle her in front of a fireplace. And exchange more searing kisses. The memory of how she'd tasted left him hard and wanting.

It was a damned inconvenient feeling, seated as he was with her overprotective guardians on either side. And he still hadn't sorted out his emotional state. While part of him could understand why Arden hadn't come after him to tell him about the baby, he was still furious. A man had a right to know if he was a father. *Or if he wasn't.*

"Frost?" Justin's voice was sharp, and Garrett realized Arden's brother was trying to hand him the plate of bread slices.

"Thanks." He took a piece and passed the plate along to Colin.

Arden looked from Garrett to her eldest brother. "You two have a lot in common. Cows, sheep, horses. Colin is a large-animal veterinarian."

Garrett wondered if the aloof man was better with animals than people. "That so?" he asked, not sure where he was supposed to take conversation from here. He struggled to think whether any of the heifers in the Double F herd had demonstrated any symptoms he could ask about. In the Frost household, Caroline didn't stand for any discussion of parasites or erosive lesions at the dinner table, but desperate times called for desperate measures.

"Was," Colin said. "I was a large-animal vet, but I'm scaling back to more generalized services."

Arden froze with her fork halfway to her mouth. Her speared piece of lasagna fell to the plate with a gooey splat. "What do you mean, more generalized?"

"Traveling. Doing odd jobs on ranches. I've got plenty of contacts throughout the state." Colin shrugged, not meeting her eyes. "You knew I was making some changes."

"But I thought they'd be local changes—that you'd find somewhere else to live in Cielo Peak, maybe resume your practice someday." Agitated, she swiveled her head toward Justin. Was she checking to see if he'd known about this, or imploring him to intervene?

Although Justin took a more subtle, playful approach

in his response, he didn't seem any happier than his sister. "If you go on walkabout, who's gonna keep me and her out of trouble?"

Colin made a short, bleak noise that Garrett belatedly identified as a laugh. Or a mutated cousin of one, anyway. "It's been a long time since I was able to take care of anyone. I'll stay until the baby's born, but then…" He changed the subject, putting Garrett on the spot. "What about you? Will you be staying in Cielo Peak much longer, or heading back to your own ranch?"

Good question. "I haven't decided. I came here planning to stay a week, but I may have to extend that."

"Must not be very important on that ranch if they can spare you so easily," Justin said.

"Justin Alexander!" Arden sounded very much like a mom, making Garrett grin. "You will not be rude to my guest under my roof."

Instead of looking shamed, the man turned to Garrett. "Any chance I could persuade you to finish this conversation under my roof? A whole different set of rules apply there."

Garrett ignored him, focusing instead on Arden, who'd seemed so distraught over her brother's leaving. Over losing another person. "I can't stay in Cielo Peak indefinitely, but I'll figure out a way to be here for the birth," he said quietly. He could give a rat's ass what Justin or Colin thought of him, but he wanted Arden to know he wouldn't desert her.

She swallowed. "That could be hard to plan ahead. The doctors are estimating November thirtieth, but due dates are notoriously unreliable. Especially for first-time mothers."

Not to mention that having surgery to remove a kidney could seriously decrease Garrett's mobility. But those were details to be hashed out later, when he had more information. "I saw the brochures on your counter. Do you need a partner for those birth classes?"

She hesitated. "Technically, my friend Layla is signed up to go with me."

"And if she hadn't, I was going to," Justin said with a thin smile. "So we've got it covered."

"Oh, please!" Arden rounded on him. "Weren't your exact words last week *no way in hell?* I wouldn't let you come with me to scam on vulnerable women."

"I don't do anything of the sort," Justin protested. "I may not be looking for anything long-term, but *I* don't exploit women." He slanted Garrett a glance that made his fists curl.

Garrett hadn't exploited anyone. Hell, he was the wronged party here.

"I want to be involved," he told Arden stiffly. "This is my child, too." He wasn't sure yet how they would make the situation work from two different parts of the state, but being some faceless, distant entity in his own kid's life was not an option.

The brothers Cade exchanged significant looks. Apparently, neither of them appreciated his asserting paternal rights. Their hostility was beginning to goad Garrett past polite behavior.

Colin leaned forward, his body language aggressive. "I don't have much family left. Arden means the world to me. I hope you'll forgive my old-fashioned heavy-handedness when I say, you'd damn well better not hurt her."

How dare they act as if he was the bad guy? "I would never physically harm a woman, but you may have meant emotionally. Something along the lines of betraying her, maybe? Keeping secrets? Lying to her about the most important event of her life?" he snapped. "No, I wouldn't do *that* to anyone, either."

"Garrett." Arden's feather-soft voice was full of pain and remorse. All three men heard the tears quavering in her tone.

Justin was out of his chair in an instant. "You son of a—"

"No! He's right," Arden said. "I think Garrett and I should talk alone."

"Leave you alone with the jerk making you cry?" Justin demanded. "What kind of brother would do that?"

"The kind who is respecting his sister's wishes," Colin said wearily, getting to his feet. "We've met him, we know what he looks like. If we need to find him to kick his ass at some future date, we will."

This time Garrett held his tongue. He was too glad to see them go to take the bait. And he regretted his impulsive outburst. He hated to see Arden cry, and it wasn't in his nature to lash out at a pregnant woman. But the anger was a fresh wound. Had it only been yesterday that he learned the earth-shattering truth? His temper had been simmering, and Arden's brothers had provoked him past reason.

With the two men gone, silence permeated the room like a dense, chilly fog. *What now?* The night he'd met Arden Cade, everything between them had happened so naturally. He'd never felt so instantly connected to anyone else. This ironic reversal of fortunes would have been laughable if it weren't so maddening.

"I should apologize for my brothers," she began tentatively.

Garrett expelled a heavy breath. "No. You aren't responsible for their actions, only yours."

She began shredding her paper napkin into tiny pieces. "And that's the problem, isn't it? My actions. Or inaction."

"Yes," he said bluntly. There were a lot of things to like about Arden, but none of them erased her selfish decision. He wasn't sure he'd be able to completely forgive her. If he hadn't happened to be in the grocery store at that exact moment, she could have kept her secret indefinitely.

There would have been a child in the world who was *his* and he never would have known.

He would have missed birthdays and recitals and graduations. Illnesses, homework struggles, dating advice. Garrett had been raised to believe there was nothing more important than family and, at a time when he needed that anchor more than ever before, Arden would have taken his own flesh and blood from him.

She said she wanted what was best for her child. Had she really believed that raising the kid with no father, with unanswered questions and secrets, was better than letting Garrett be a part of their lives? The sting of that was indescribable.

"You must hate me." Her words were thick with self-recrimination.

"No. Whatever I feel for you…it's a lot more complex than that." It wasn't an easy admission. Understanding his reaction to her was difficult enough in his own mind, much less out loud. He began clearing dishes from the table.

"You don't have to do that."

"This is what I've been trying to tell you—I *want* to help. I want to be a decent father." And he didn't want to harden into this angry, unrecognizable version of himself. He wasn't sure how to forgive Arden. Or his mother. Or Will. But the alternative… He turned on the hot water. "I realize your brothers despise me, but I'm glad I met them. Colin was something of a wake-up call. I found something out last week that destroyed my view of the world. I've been very…bitter ever since. Cut off from the people in my life. Even though you love your brother, and vice versa, he's isolated. I don't want to be like that."

"He's damaged," she agreed, fighting a sob. "And God, I wish I knew how to help him."

Garrett rinsed the dishes wordlessly. The pat answer was that she had to give her brother time, but how did he know that would work? He'd never faced losses of such magnitude. How much time was enough?

He felt Arden watching him, wondered what she was thinking. That he'd ruined her family dinner, perhaps?

"This thing you found out," she asked, "was it about your mother?"

"Yes." Was he ready to share something so personal? *She's having your baby, it doesn't get much more personal than that.* He scrubbed a plate with escalating force. "My mother had an affair thirty-one years ago. My dad—Brandon Frost, the man I know as my dad— isn't really my father."

"That must have been hard. But it doesn't change the relationship you have with him. Does it?"

"Not in theory, but she still hasn't told him the truth. I don't know how to be around him, lying to his face day in and day out. The only reason she finally told me is because my biological father is dying." It was the first time he'd said the words aloud, and the severity of the situation struck him anew.

"Oh, Garrett. Do you know him?"

"He's a family friend. He spent a couple of Christmases with us here and there, sent me a check for way too much money as a high school graduation gift." Which made a lot more sense in retrospect. "He has diabetes, and his condition has messed up his kidneys. He needs a transplant. My mother told me about him because she wants me to consider giving him one of mine."

Arden's gasp was audible.

He shot her a grim smile over his shoulder. "See? You're not the only one with family drama."

WHILE GARRETT FINISHED with the dishes, Arden excused herself to the restroom. It was a lame attempt to get a few minutes by herself and collect her scattered composure. Was there a single emotion she hadn't experienced tonight? She sat on the edge of the bathtub, trying to find her balance. She'd been off-kilter since Garrett kissed her, unprepared for the enormity of her desire. The chemistry between them certainly hadn't dimmed over the months.

Once her brothers had arrived, she'd felt both gratitude for their concern and outrage at the way they'd treated Garrett. She'd gone through dismay and sympathy and shock. *And guilt.* The guilt was staggering.

In the past few days, she'd witnessed Garrett act with honor and periodic tenderness. Despite any hard feelings he harbored toward her, he was a gentleman, one willing to face up to his responsibilities. Embrace them, even. Maternal instinct told her he would make an excellent father. And she'd almost denied him that.

Her time with her own parents had been cut unforgivably short—what would she give for another day with her dad? Yet she would have sacrificed her child's time with Garrett.

"Arden?" There was a soft knock at the door. "I don't mean to intrude, but I was starting to worry."

Good hostesses didn't hide from their guests. "I'm fine." Physically. Mentally, she was a wreck. "Out in a minute."

Listening to his retreating footsteps, she closed her eyes and tried to relax by counting to ten and doing some meditative breathing. Deeming her efforts pointless, she gave up and joined Garrett in the living room.

"If I ever invite you to my house for a dinner party again, remind me that I suck at this, okay?"

"Oh, I've had worse evenings." He steepled his fingers beneath his chin. "There was a night I got salmonella poisoning at a county fair. And then there was that incident with a bull who'd been incorrectly tethered at an auction barn."

It was miraculous that, with all she'd put him through in the past twenty-four hours, *he* was trying to make *her* feel better. She sat next to him on the sofa, trying to ignore his now-familiar scent. "I wanted this to go differently. I wanted us to…" Her body tingled with the memory of his kiss. If only things between them could be as simple as finding sanctuary in each other's arms. "To be friends." She wanted to ask if that was possible but was afraid of his answer.

"I have an OB appointment Friday afternoon," she continued. "There's no sonogram or anything. The most interesting thing about the whole visit is that I have to drink a solution for the glucose screen beforehand but if you want to come…"

"I'd love to."

Feeling that she was offering too little, too late, she was driven by a need to include him in as many baby preparations as possible. "Would you be hopelessly bored going with me to shop for the nursery this weekend? For months, I didn't really buy any baby stuff because I was paranoid about something going wrong and too queasy to move. Then when I got my energy back, I was so focused on making up for lost time at work that I never got around to registering. I have portrait sessions at the studio all morning Saturday, and the high school hired me to take pictures at the homecoming ball Saturday night, but I'm free Sunday."

"Then it's a date. But after Sunday, I'll have to leave town. At least for a few days."

"To check on the ranch?"

"Yes." He looked away, the tension lining his face making her feel protective. She wanted to smooth his brow and soothe his troubles. "And to set up a couple of medical appointments of my own."

"Because of your fa— That man you told me about? You've decided to help him?"

"I don't even if know if I'm a good candidate," he said noncommittally. "Finding that out is probably step one. I don't know what will happen next."

His words resonated with her. Never knowing what came next was the story of her life.

ON THURSDAY, ARDEN met Layla for lunch at a barbecue place down the street from the school. Her friend had called the night before, as promised, but by the time Layla got home from her PTA event, Arden had been too drained to discuss her evening. But Layla had been off-campus for a meeting that morning and was free for lunch before her next class.

"So?" Layla pounced as soon as Arden walked into the restaurant. "I want to hear everything."

"Shouldn't we order our food first?" Arden asked. "You should eat before you get back to the school."

"This is my planning period." Layla rubbed her hands together. "I have almost an hour." But she waited patiently, allowing non-Garrett-related small talk while they walked to the register and placed their orders.

Arden struggled to hold up her end of the conversation. The second or third time she lost her train of thought, Layla frowned.

"Rough night, or is hunger sapping your mental energy? You don't seem yourself," her friend observed.

"It's been a…challenging morning." She'd love to vent about her earlier photo session from hell, but not with other townspeople in earshot. It was bad for business to publicly bash the clientele.

"You snag us a table," Layla directed. "I'll fill our cups."

Arden took the plastic tent marker with their number on it and sank into one of the only empty booths, right next to the window. The sunshine streaming through the glass made it seem like a much warmer day than it was. Unfortunately, the brightness only added to the discomfort in Arden's throbbing head. She massaged her temple with her thumb, hoping her afternoon clients weren't as difficult as this morning's.

She'd met with Mrs. Merriweather, a woman who wanted to surprise her husband with framed pictures of herself for his birthday. Normally, Arden tried several different backgrounds and cameras along with a variety of poses, so that the customer ultimately had plenty of options for purchase. But Mrs. Merriweather had argued about everything from the "unflattering" light to the way she was positioned. Early on in the process, she'd asked about Arden's own husband and when Arden answered that she was single, Mrs. Merriweather had glanced pointedly at Arden's stomach and sniffed in disdain.

By the time Arden left the studio for lunch, she was feeling a lot of pity for the unseen Mr. Merriweather.

"Here you go." Layla set a drink in front of her. "Food should be out soon. Sometimes getting a bite to eat helps when I have a headache."

"Thanks. I guess dealing with an opinionated client all morning was too much to take on top of not being able to sleep last night."

"Does it make you feel better to know you weren't alone?" Layla's smile was impish. "I couldn't sleep, either. The curiosity about how your dinner went was eating me alive!"

"Dinner was a fiasco. My brothers were complete asses." Annoyance flared again, but it was tempered with worry. "Colin's leaving town. I knew he was selling his place, but I thought he'd find something smaller, without so many memories. He's talking about looking for ranch work. It doesn't sound like he has a real plan, just some haphazard idea of jumping on his motorcycle and seeing where he ends up."

"Maybe that's what he needs," Layla said cautiously. "Grieving is a process everyone goes through differently."

"He told me he'll stick around 'til the baby's born. Garrett wants to be here for the birth, too. He's going with me to a doctor's appointment tomorrow."

"So you two are on friendly terms?"

Did wanting to tear his clothes off in her kitchen count as friendly? That had been the high point of the night, but there had been a lot of turmoil after that. "I've damaged his trust," she said somberly. "I don't know if it will be possible for us to ever be close. And the sexual awareness is confusing."

"Confusing? He's a hot cowboy. From where I sit, the sexual awareness makes total sense."

"That's not—" She paused when the waitress came over with a tray of food.

"Here you are, ladies. One pulled pork spud with a side salad, one sandwich plate. Enjoy!" Her smile dimmed suddenly, and Arden followed her gaze. Justin was walking toward their table.

After the waitress beat a speedy retreat, Arden rolled her eyes. "Don't tell me," she said to her approaching brother. "You dated her briefly."

He squirmed, not meeting her gaze. "It didn't end as amicably as I'd hoped. Hi, Layla. Mind if I take a seat?"

"Don't you dare!" Arden interrupted before her friend could reply. "I shouldn't even be speaking to you after that ridiculous, chest-beating macho display last night."

"I did not beat my chest," he countered. "The rest of it…may be accurate."

"Go find your own table. Better yet, find Garrett. And apologize."

"Returning to my classroom to conjugate verbs with sophomores is going to be really dull after this," Layla said to no one in particular.

"Sounds dull no matter when you do it." Justin hitched his thumbs in his front pockets, adopting a contrite expression. "Look, Arden, I'm not about to apologize to Frost. But if I did anything to upset you—"

"If?" she squeaked.

"I'll, uh, just let you two continue your lunch," he backtracked. "We'll talk later, sis."

As he shuffled off in search of a seat, Layla chortled. "It always cracks me up to see you put your brothers in their place. It's like watching a kitten scold a rottweiler."

"Kitten?" Arden echoed dubiously. "More like a hippo. I've never felt so ungainly." Part of the magic in Garrett's kiss last night was that, even while she hadn't been able to get as close as she'd wanted, with the baby wedged between them, he'd made her feel sexy as hell. She hadn't felt bulky or undesirable in the slightest.

"Penny for your thoughts."

"Nope." Arden doubted a penny was the going rate for adult pay-per-view, and that seemed to be the direction her mind was headed. Lusting after him was futile. She wasn't sure they could achieve friendship, much less anything more. But with her body chemistry all out of whack and the knowledge of just how good she and Garrett were together, it was difficult to keep her longing in check.

She rubbed her temple again, glad her afternoon was booked solid. It would keep her too busy to dwell on this unwise attraction or to worry about her oldest brother.

But, several hours later, as Arden's headache was evolving into a full-blown migraine, she felt less grateful for her afternoon lineup, especially Mrs. Tucker's twins. The three-year-old girls were…well, monsters. No other word was adequate.

When they were asleep, they were probably adorable. Seeing them through the front window in their matching houndstooth dresses with brightly colored pockets, collars and belts, Arden had experienced a misguided instant when she thought they were cute. A fleeting notion. Before they were fully inside the studio, problems erupted. Odette, who didn't want to have her picture taken, had gone limp. Mrs. Tucker literally had to drag the child through the door. Meanwhile, the other twin, Georgette, was screaming that Odette had taken her purple crayon. The accusations were delivered at the highest possible decibel level and punctuated with flying fists. She pulsed with rage. Arden wondered if three-year-olds could have strokes.

"Could you watch her for just a moment?" the beleaguered Mrs. Tucker asked with a nod to Odette. "I'm going to take Georgie into the restroom to wipe her face and fix her hair before we get started." The little girl's red-and-yellow bow had been no match for her hurricane of temper.

As soon as Mrs. Tucker was out of sight, Odette lodged herself beneath a heavy train table Arden kept in the lobby for children. "No pick-sures!" the girl shrieked.

Arden's skull felt as if it were being squeezed in a vise. Her chest hurt, and the self-doubt that welled up within her was suffocating. What if her child was exactly like this? Would Arden know how to correct the situation lovingly, or would she overreact and set a bad example? Would she become like Mrs. Tucker, with her glazed eyes and resigned air of defeat?

By the time Mrs. Tucker wrestled both of her daughters in front of the backdrop, their dresses were askew, neither of them had hair bows anymore and Georgie's nose was running steadily.

"Um..." Arden peered through the camera and absently adjusted some settings, but nothing she did was going to make this a picture worth purchasing. "Would you rather do this on another day Mrs. Tucker? I'm flexible."

The woman gaped. "Are you *crazy?* Do you know what I had to go through just to get them here in the first place? I am not going through that again." She jabbed a finger at Arden's protruding abdomen, as implacable as the Ghost of Christmas Future pointing to the grave. "You'll understand soon enough."

Chapter Seven

"You don't look so good." Garrett regretted the words even as they were leaving his mouth. Why would he say something so stupid? He blamed a late night of researching organ donation until his eyes had crossed. Giving Arden a sheepish smile, he jerked his thumb over his shoulder, toward the lobby. "How about I step out, then come back in and start over?"

Her chuckle was wan. "Not necessary. I don't kick people out of my office for telling the truth."

His offer to pick her up for the OB appointment had been twofold—he was serious about them getting to know each other better, and it seemed silly to take more than one vehicle. But it also seemed lucky that he was here since she looked too tired to drive herself. He wouldn't be surprised if she fell asleep on the way to the doctor's office.

"Are you okay?" he asked. "No more fainting spells?"

"Nothing like that," she assured him, rising from her desk chair. "I just had a rough day at work yesterday, followed by the headache that wouldn't die. My medicinal options are limited now that I'm pregnant, and I was too uncomfortable to sleep."

"I wish you'd called me," he said, not sure why he

made the rash statement. What would have been accomplished by her calling? Chatting on the phone wouldn't have been fun for someone with a killer headache, and it wasn't as if he could have lullabied her to sleep. Garrett did not sing. The world was a better place for it.

Her expression mirrored his own incredulity. "You do?"

"Dumb, huh? I'd just like to feel useful. While I'm in town, feel free to phone day or night. If your heart starts racing too fast again or if you want someone to bring you pickles and ice cream." When she made a face at the silly cliché, he added, "Not literally. I meant, any craving you have that I could help satisfy."

Her eyes widened, and he reconsidered his words.

"Food cravings." Although, now that his mind had started down that path… Arden had confessed that one of her recent pregnancy symptoms was amplified desire. How would he respond if she called him in the middle of the night, her voice husky with need, and—

"W-we have to go." Her face was a brighter red than the scarlet mallow wildflowers that blossomed near the ranch every summer. "I already drank that sugar solution, and I need to reach the office at a certain time for the test to be valid."

"Right. After you." He almost felt guilty about his undisciplined lust, but he knew it was mutual. The way she'd kissed him a couple of days ago… *Dammit, Frost, pull yourself together.* This was a medical appointment, not a third date.

While they walked to his truck, he apologized for being distracted, hoping he could play it off as sleep deprivation rather than ill-timed sexual fantasizing. "As it happens, I didn't get much rest last night, either. I read living donor FAQs and articles about Colorado transplant centers into the wee hours." When he'd finally hit the pillow, terms like *laparoscopic* and *antigen match* had continued to swirl behind his eyelids.

"It must be daunting, the idea of going through such a physical ordeal."

He opened her door, shaking his head wryly. "Says the woman soon to have a baby?" A kidney was a lot smaller than an infant. And, *if* he went through with it, he'd get to be unconscious for the whole thing.

He was fastening his seat belt when he noticed Arden nibbling at her bottom lip, drawing his attention to her mouth. A man could get lost there.

"Something on your mind?" he prompted.

"Sort of. It's none of my business, though."

"We're becoming better acquainted, remember? I'm interested in your opinion."

"After I found out I was pregnant, I went on this information binge. I marked a bunch of sites on the internet, bought a stack of books, started DVRing this documentary-style show that follows expectant mothers. But none of those resources could give me what I really needed. Deep down, I wasn't looking for stats on fetal development and the most popular baby names, I was looking for peace of mind. Acceptance of the situation. It's commendable that you're doing your homework, preparing yourself with facts, but I don't think sites on renal transplants will give you the answers you're looking for."

He tightened his grip on the steering wheel. Could *anything* give him the peace of mind she mentioned?

He knew he had to talk to his mother, but whenever he mentally rehearsed the conversation, it spiraled into disjointed recriminations. They'd only communicated through texts since he'd arrived in Cielo Peak.

"You want to know the horrible truth?" he asked quietly. "A big part of me hopes I'm not a good match, because then the decision's out of my hands. I don't want to deal with these mixed emotions about my dad or Mom or Will. Cowardly, isn't it?"

"Human," she amended, blessing him with unconditional compassion. "You've had so much dumped on you in the past, what, week and a half? It's mind-boggling. Don't beat yourself up over needing time to process it. I've watched people deal with bad shocks before, and it can involve anything from going catatonic to drinking too much and picking bar fights. The way you're handling everything is…amazing."

"Thank you. And thank you for listening. I tried to tell Hugh about some of this, but couldn't quite put it all into words." Despite Wednesday's awkward silences, maybe Garrett's initial impression of her had been right, after all. "You're very easy to talk to."

She sniffled, diverting his gaze from the road as he checked on her.

"Did I say something wrong?" he asked in alarm.

"No. You made me think of Natalie. Her willingness to listen was one of my favorite things about her. There was nothing you couldn't tell her, and I miss that so much. It was major praise, hearing that someone saw a bit of that same quality in me." She fluttered her fingers in front of her eyes, as if that might stop her from getting weepy. He wasn't sure he followed the logic behind the action. "This is ridiculous. I'm crying at everything lately. I sobbed over a banner ad on a recipe site the other day."

He laughed, hoping she wasn't offended. It wasn't mocking laughter. The truth was, he found her sentimentality kind of adorable.

"Turn left up here," she instructed.

"So is the crying strictly a pregnancy thing?" he asked. "I mean, are you someone who normally needs a box of tissues during a sad movie, or is this just a hormone-based anomaly?"

"I'd love to say I'm usually tough, but I'm not. Pregnancy is magnifying everything about me. I've been known to cry at soup commercials. At least those are thirty seconds of actual story, with endearing characters. Banner ads are a new low! The sad-movie question is moot, though. I try to avoid them. What the heck's wrong with happy endings? We could use more of those in film and in real life."

Her wistful tone pierced him, making him want to shield her from any more sadness. She'd said *he* was amazing for coping? Honestly, this was the first time in his life he'd been tested. He'd always been healthy, had lived in a home with loving parents and had done perfectly well in school. He'd never loved anyone enough to propose, but he'd never been lonely or suffered through a traumatic breakup, either. Arden, on the other hand... She was only twenty-five, and she'd had to survive enough upheaval for two lifetimes.

"You need to get in the right lane before the next light," she said.

"Got it." He flipped on his blinker. "So, no sad movies. Comedies, then?"

"Actually, I'm a sucker for action movies. Possibly because I grew up in a house full of guys. I'll take the original *Die Hard* over the majority of chick flicks. And I like the action stuff with a science-fiction angle."

Arden kept navigating, but between directions, they exchanged DVD recommendations and got into a spirited debate over which sequel in a futuristic spy franchise was the worst. By the time he parked in front of the medical building, she was in much higher spirits than when he'd first arrived at her office. Her eyes sparkled with humor as she facetiously tried to convince him the hilariously bad '90s flop *Vengeance Before Breakfast* was the best movie of all time. Did she know how beautiful she was when she smiled liked that?

She stopped abruptly in the middle of her animated grenade-scene reenactment. "You're staring. You know I was kidding about it being a great movie, right?"

"Didn't mean to stare. I'm just glad to see you're feeling better. No more pinched look around your eyes, and you got your color back." Leaning toward her, he traced his finger up the slope of her cheek. Her skin was silky beneath his touch. *What are you doing?* He dropped his hand. "We should get inside."

A long interior hallway led them to her doctor's practice. Garrett opened the door for her, then hesitated, feeling unexpectedly like an invader in a foreign land. Surely it was normal for fathers-to-be to attend some of these appointments, but today, he was the only guy. Women of all ages, shapes and sizes sat beneath huge framed black-and-white photos. Some of the poster-size shots focused on a pregnant belly, others were of mommies cuddling newborns. The carpet was pale pink, and the chairs were cushioned in an assortment of pastel colors.

He was overwhelmed with a clawing need to run out and buy power tools. Or work on his truck.

Instead, he followed Arden to the check-in window, where she let the woman behind the counter know the exact time she'd ingested her test solution. The receptionist said someone would take her back momentarily to draw her blood, but then she'd have to return to the waiting room until an exam room was available.

"We're pretty busy today," the woman added unnecessarily.

They weren't able to find two unoccupied chairs next to each other, but a woman in her mid-fifties scooted over to make room for Garrett. He gave her a grateful smile.

"Sorry about the wait," Arden told him. "But at least I got to drink that syrupy stuff before we came. When Natalie was pregnant with Danny, she had to drink at the doctor's office, then wait a whole other hour after her appointment. I would have felt awful for making you sit here that long."

In spite of his earlier discomfort, he heard himself say, "There are worse ways to spend time than an extra hour with you." It should have been light, teasing, but it came out wrong. His voice was too sincere. The fact that he couldn't tear his gaze away from hers wasn't helping.

Her face flushed a soft, becoming pink.

The sight knocked loose a piece of trivia in his mind,

and he grunted in acknowledgement. "Huh. You blushed earlier, and it brought to mind a scarlet mallow. I just remembered the other name for that flower. Cowboy's delight." Disturbingly appropriate.

"Arden Cade?" A woman with a clipboard called Arden's name over the drone of conversations taking place.

"I'll be right back." Arden stood, slow to break eye contact. As if she didn't want to leave him. Not that it was much of a compliment that she'd rather stay with him than have a needle stuck in her arm.

The older woman who'd changed chairs for him struck up conversation. "First-time parents?"

He laughed. "Is it that obvious? She's read a bunch of books, but I don't have a clue what I'm doing."

"My husband was the same way. Don't think he'd ever held a baby until our first was born. He for darn sure had never changed a diaper. Parenting is all about on-the-job training. You'll do fine. Just love her and love the little one. Be patient with her for the rest of the pregnancy—it gets worse before it gets better. But the first time that infant's tiny fingers wrap around yours, you'll know it's all worth it."

He nodded weakly, even though he felt a little sick inside. On-the-job training? He might not have that opportunity. How were they going to handle custody? He would never challenge Arden's right to raise their child, but he didn't want his son or daughter to only see him on holidays and periodic weekends. Would she be willing to move? It would be a major life change—and she had her brothers to consider—but, in theory, she could take pictures anywhere. He couldn't very well bring one hundred head of cattle to an apartment in Cielo Peak.

He looked forward to teaching his son or daughter to ride horses, to show them around the ranch where he'd spent his entire life, the land that was in his blood. Loving his child would be easy. He was already half-smitten, and the birth was months away. But loving Arden? After what she'd done? The stranger meant well, but her counsel wasn't applicable in his situation.

To discourage further conversation, he grabbed a magazine off the nearby end table, opened to a random page and tried to look engrossed. His thoughts were racing, and he didn't even see the words printed in front of him. Nor did he notice Arden's return.

"Wow," she said, craning her head to see what he'd been reading. "I didn't know you were so interested in… the best remedies for hair-coloring disasters?"

"What?" He shut the magazine, and bold purple type on the cover caught his eye. "'Thirty-six ways to please him in bed?' Damn, are they overthinking that. You want to please a guy in bed, show up."

That startled a giggle out of her. She covered her hand with her mouth, as if embarrassed, and sat down. "Just show up? Sounds pretty passive."

"I don't remember you being the least bit passive, sweetheart."

She didn't blush or turn away. Those blue-green eyes locked on his as she tilted her body toward him and lowered her voice. "No, I wasn't, was I? As soon as you put your arms around me on that dance floor, I knew what I wanted and went for it."

Heat flooded him, shooting directly to his groin. Was kissing her in the middle of the reception area a bad idea?

Arden nibbled her bottom lip. "Can I ask you something?"

"Yes." *Whatever you want.* He'd give her the keys to his truck right now.

"Why me?" She spoke just above a whisper, and he had to get closer to catch every word. "That night…I'd never done anything like that before." She looked down, toying with a loose thread at the hem of her coat. "Is it normal for you? I have brothers. I know men have casual sex, I just…"

He was as charmed by her sudden shyness as he had been by her boldness a moment ago. "For the record, I don't think there was anything *casual* about what happened between us. I've never slept with anyone else that quickly."

"No?" she asked hopefully.

"My best friend had just gotten married. Happy as I am for him, it was odd to think he was settling down, buying a house, eventually having kids. Meanwhile, I'd broken up with a girlfriend a few weeks before and was feeling, not lonely, exactly, but restless? Then I saw you. And I forgot about everyone else. Even though it was Hugh's reception, I would have bailed in a heartbeat if you'd gone with me."

She peered at him through her lashes. "Professional photographers don't ditch the events they're working. Bad business. But it sure would've been tempting."

"Arden Cade?"

Her head jerked up guiltily, as if the nurse had caught them doing something illicit. "That's me." She turned to Garrett. "Okay, this is the part you can come back for. We'll probably get to hear the heartbeat again."

Plus, he got to remain in her company, which was far more enticing than it should have been.

ARDEN WAS FAMILIAR with the procedure by now. First, the nurse sent her to the restroom with a cup, then took her vitals—including weight. Face warm, Arden asked Garrett if he wouldn't mind waiting farther down the hall. He smirked but did as requested. Then the nurse showed them to room number three, sliding Arden's chart into the plastic file slot on the door.

Thankfully, for the visit she had today, Arden didn't need to disrobe, but she still felt oddly exposed atop the examination table.

Her doctor was Jason Mehta, an OB whose own wife happened to be expecting. Normally he was all smiles and full of anecdotes that put Arden at ease. But today, he entered the room looking troubled. He drew up short when he spotted Garrett; this was the first time she'd ever brought anyone with her.

"I am Dr. Mehta." He extended a hand. "Pleased to meet you."

"This is Garrett," Arden said. "He's the father. I thought he might like to listen to the baby's heartbeat, hear for himself that everything's going well?" Her nervousness made the last part come out as a question. Maybe Dr. Mehta was having a stressful day and his expression didn't have anything to do with her pregnancy.

His next words ruled out that optimistic thinking. "What did the nurse tell you about your blood pressure?"

"Nothing. She wrote it down on the paper but seemed

in a hurry to get me processed. You guys have a really full lineup today."

"She must have wished me to discuss it with you, so I could allay your concerns."

Arden straightened. "There's reason for concern?"

Garrett moved from his post by the door to her side, taking her hand. His thumb brushed back and forth over her hand. She appreciated the soothing gesture, but it couldn't completely prevent her alarm.

"Let's not panic," Dr. Mehta said. "Your blood pressure's never been a problem prior to this, and it was not abnormally high going into the pregnancy. Is it possible you've been under stress lately?"

A strangled laugh escaped her. "You could say that. Plus, I've barely slept the last two nights. Didn't I read somewhere that there's a correlation between lack of sleep and elevated blood pressure?"

"So this is probably an isolated occurrence." The doctor eyed her sternly. "You, young lady, need your rest. The blood pressure spike may well prove to be nothing of consequence, but this is after your twentieth week. I would not be doing my job if I didn't ask some follow-up questions. Any nausea lately?"

"Not in weeks." On the contrary, she'd been feeling pretty good. Especially when Garrett touched her, causing a giddy buzz of sensation. She darted a sidelong glance in his direction. When he was this close, could he tell the effect he had on her?

"Any swelling?" When she glanced pointedly at her stomach, the doctor chuckled. "I meant in your extremities. What about headache?"

"She had a killer headache last night," Garrett blurted. "Why? Does that mean something?"

Dr. Mehta made a noncommittal noise, jotting notes on her chart. "Have you suffered blurred vision?"

"Well, yes, but I've had migraines in the past that frequently mess up my vision. I didn't think it was related to the baby."

"Hmmm. The good news is, there's been no protein in urine—at least, not more than the normal trace amounts."

Arden wanted to cover her face with her hands. She was more attracted to Garrett than any man in memory, and even if nothing was going to come of that, she'd rather he not be subjected to discussions about her bodily fluids. She snuck a peek at Garrett, who looked hyperalert, like a soldier at attention. As if he were memorizing everything Dr. Mehta said and avidly awaited instruction.

The doctor put a hand on her shoulder. "You are a healthy young woman. It's likely everything is fine. But you need to come back next week so we can check your blood pressure again and rule out preeclampsia. Meanwhile, to err on the side of caution, try to stay off your feet. I won't prescribe complete bed rest if you swear to me you'll take it easy."

She craned her neck to look up at Garrett. "Better cancel our nursery shopping trip for Sunday. That might be too much after a full day of work Saturday."

"What exactly does this day of work entail?" the doctor interrupted.

"I have a number of portrait sessions scheduled and

the big high school dance Saturday night. I'm the official photographer," she explained.

He scratched his chin. "And that would involve walking around and taking a bunch of candid shots in a noisy ballroom as well as being out late? Absolutely not. You should reschedule the other Saturday sessions, too. Unless you can promise me you'll be taking all the pictures from a chair without moving around much and that none of your clients are going to be demanding and in any way raise your blood pressure further."

She thought of Mrs. Merriweather and the Tucker twins. "Um…"

"That is what I thought."

"But…" Her eyes stung. "I'm a professional. I can't just flake out on everyone."

"Even professionals cancel when there is a medical necessity," Dr. Mehta said gently. "Arden, your baby needs you far more than the high school students do."

He was right. She knew he was right. But she'd already been worried about how the baby would affect her work *after* the birth. She was thrilled to become a mother, but babies weren't cheap. Photography was how she kept a roof over her head. She wasn't sure the high school administrators would be able to find anyone good on such short notice. If they did, would she be losing their future business to an unknown competitor?

She blinked rapidly, trying her damnedest not to cry in front of Garrett or the doctor. She was only able to half concentrate on the rest of what Dr. Mehta said during the visit. Thank goodness Garrett was there to help catch whatever she missed. Finally, the doctor left them, reminding her to make a follow-up appointment with the receptionist.

Garrett stepped to the edge of the table and pulled her against his chest for a comforting hug. It was exactly what she needed, but, unfortunately, she lost the battle with the tears she'd been struggling not to shed. The front of his shirt grew damp beneath her face.

"Y-you must think I'm s-so selfish, caring more about my j-job than—"

"Hush. I don't think that at all, sweetheart."

She sniffed. "I had to cut back while I was sick. Now that it's passed, I've been trying to take as many jobs as possible, to save up for—"

"Arden." He drew back so she could see his expression. "Don't worry about the money. I can help with that. What I can't do is keep this baby any safer. I know we haven't talked specifics yet—hell, this time last week, I didn't even know you were pregnant—but Peanut is my responsibility, too. No, not just responsibility. My *gift,* too."

She was dazed by his generous spirit. Not the financial generosity, but his emotional openness. Some men would be demanding a paternity test right about now to make sure the kid was even theirs before offering to pay a dime. She knew from his candor Wednesday night how angry Garrett was, yet he was at her side, hugging her. And when he talked about the baby, there was real caring in his voice.

Guilt seized her, raw and wrenching. This wasn't how parenthood should have begun for him. It should have been with someone he loved. She could easily imagine his joy at hearing the news for the first time.

He probably would've brought flowers for the woman, a big floppy teddy bear for the baby. He should have been there from day one, and she could never give that back to him.

She swallowed hard. "I need to go pay and set up that appointment. Heaven knows they need the room back."

"If you need another minute, they can wait," he said gruffly.

"I'm good." It was a lie, but one designed to put him at ease. She realized she was feeling as protective of him as he sounded about her.

They returned to the front of the building and arranged her next visit. She almost asked Garrett if he would come with her but bit her tongue. He'd mentioned that he would need to leave Cielo Peak. His entire life was elsewhere, and he had pressing concerns of his own. He couldn't drop everything to hold her hand.

Both of them were quiet on the ride back to her studio. Arden was dreading the phone calls she needed to make, rehearsing what she would say to the clients she was about to disappoint. "Rescheduling the individual sessions shouldn't be too bad," she mused aloud. "I can offer them a big discount for their inconvenience. It's losing the high school business that bothers me. All the future potential—yearbook photos, prom, graduation."

"I wish to God I knew the first thing about cameras. I'd go in your place," he vowed.

She smiled despite her sour mood. "You've already gone above and beyond the call of duty."

He snapped his fingers. "You mentioned yearbooks. Don't high schools usually have student staff, kids who take pictures for the yearbook and student newspaper?

Maybe several of them could cover the event for, I don't know, extra credit or something. I realize they'd be amateur pictures, but if the school uses more than one person, there could be a decent assortment of photos to choose from."

Plus, she wouldn't be handing a competitor her job on a silver platter. Bonus. "It's worth at least mentioning to the principal," she agreed. "Or maybe I could broach the suggestion with the journalism teacher first. I kind of know her a little, since Jus—"

"Let me guess. Your brother dated her?"

"You catch on quick."

"What is he, pathological?"

Truthfully, she couldn't tell if Justin was afraid of being alone or afraid of being with someone. Or both. But it seemed traitorous to discuss her brother's flaws with Garrett. "Anyway, I'll call the teacher when I get back to the studio. If I can get her jazzed up about your suggestion, she might help me convince the principal. Thank you—it's a really good idea."

"Wanna see if I can go two for two?" Garrett gave her a winning smile. "I have another great idea. Promise you'll hear me out before you answer?"

"Sure." She owed him that much.

"Come to the Double F with me."

"What?" It was the last thing she'd expected, an invitation to meet his family and see the homestead. Was he serious?

"Assuming that it's okay with your doctor, I can take you there for a long weekend. Maybe bring you back Tuesday. You're going to be miserable, canceling all your jobs this weekend, and I hate to think about you cooped up in your house, worried about that next appointment. Aren't fresh air and open spaces healthy? You'll come back rejuvenated with a suitably lowered blood pressure."

She laughed at his coaxing. "You know that for a fact?"

"I know I'll be worried about you the whole weekend if I can't check on you for myself," he admitted. "You have to see the place sometime. However we decide to manage this, our child *is* going to spend time there, right?"

"Yes." The word nearly got lodged at the back of her throat. There was no question that Garrett deserved time with the baby, but the thought of being separated even briefly stabbed right through her. For six months, this baby had been entirely hers. She already loved it more than anything in the world.

"You're too good a mother to let your kid stay somewhere you'd haven't already assessed," he said matter-of-factly. "So come with me now, before the baby's born and your schedule gets even more hectic. Who knows? Maybe you'll fall in love with the place."

Her worst fear—falling in love with yet one more thing she couldn't hold on to. One more thing that would break her heart.

NEITHER OF THE Connors was home when Garrett returned from dropping Arden off at work. He'd told her to call him when she was on the way home this evening so he could meet her at the house. "I'll help pack," he'd insisted. "You can supervise. From a comfy spot with your feet propped up and a glass of water in your hand." His tone had brooked no argument.

She'd groused some choice phrases about "high-handed males" but she'd agreed. After all, they both had the same goal—protecting the little one.

Using the spare key Darcy had lent him, Garrett let himself inside, thinking that it was probably best his hosts couldn't see him now. In spite of everything, he was grinning like an idiot. Knowing that Arden would be on his ranch, the land he'd loved since he was a boy, filled him with a sense of triumph and more joy than was strictly logical. As soon as he'd first wondered if she might one day agree to move, he'd been steadily consumed with a need to show her the Double F.

She was emotional right now, and he could imagine how a conversation where he asked her to uproot her entire life would go. It would simplify matters if she'd already grown fond of the area surrounding his home. Relocating might give their unorthodox family their only legitimate chance at bonding. Maybe he was getting ahead of himself, but it was invigorating to nurture some small spark of optimism in the pit of confusion his life had become.

Unfortunately, there was one thing he had to do before he took Arden to the ranch. He had to call his mom. So far, he'd responded to her texts but had managed to put off actually speaking to her. In every message she sent, he could feel her anxiety like a sunburn abrading his skin.

If he called the house now, his father would probably be outside, still working for the day. Assuming Caroline was home, she should be at liberty to talk. Should he practice what to say? Bitterness swamped him. He'd been raised on the propaganda that he and his parents could talk to each other about anything, yet now he had to rehearse just to endure a ten-minute phone call with his own mother?

Best to get this over with, then. Sitting at the Connors' kitchen table, he pulled his phone out of his pocket. He was up and pacing before the first ring had finished.

"Garrett? Oh, thank God." Her voice was full of maternal reproach. It made him crazy that, in spite of the position she'd put him in, *she* could make *him* feel guilty. "I've been worried sick!"

"It wasn't my intent to worry you by not calling," he said stiffly. "I told you I needed space. But I'll be coming home tomorrow, at least temporarily. If you talk to Will—" damn, those words were hard to say "—tell him that I've made a preliminary appointment consultation. My understanding is that's followed by up to a week in the hospital with testing to find out if I'm a good candidate. That's not to say I've decided one hundred percent to go through with the procedure even if I am, but—"

"It's a start. We're both so sorry to have to put you through—"

"Don't!" He didn't want to think about his mom and Will as a unified "we." The idea of the two of them, his *parents,* discussing him behind Brandon's back... His free hand clenched into a fist. Knowing he couldn't hurt granite, he took a swing at Darcy's countertop. It stung like a bitch, but left him feeling calmer. "There's something else I need to tell you. I'm bringing someone with me to the ranch. A woman named Arden Cade."

"Oh?" Beneath the expected surprise was a note of what sounded like disapproval.

"Is that a problem?" he asked defensively. He was a grown man with his own house on the acreage. He'd had overnight guests and weekend visitors over the years.

"Garrett, you're in a very tough place right now. Not quite yourself, and I don't want you doing anything drastic that you might regret later. I know a lot about regrets," she murmured. "Knee-jerk reactions to stress and jumping into—"

"I do not want your advice on relationships." He also didn't want to argue with her or listen to more apologies. "I'll text you before we hit the road. See you tomorrow."

He hung up the phone, angry with his own rudeness and her hypocrisy. He wasn't fourteen, looking for her wisdom on girls. How could she act as if their mother-son dynamic hadn't been irreparably altered?

If he hadn't gotten so ticked off, maybe he could have done a better job explaining his and Arden's situation. *Or not.* The righteous fury that had burned through him when he learned about his child was still there, boiling below the surface like lava, but other powerful feelings were developing, too. The instinct to shield her and the baby from all harm. The driving need to kiss her again. The appreciation for her inviting nature— when he wasn't actively angry with her, she was easier to talk to than almost anyone he knew.

The more time he spent with Arden Cade, the less he understood just what their situation was. Now they'd be together for three days in his one-bedroom home. Would he come out of this weekend with answers? Or just more questions?

Chapter Eight

Arden stared out the truck window, suppressing the need to ask for another stop this soon after the last one. Garrett's parents were expecting them for lunch. *At the rate we're traveling, we might make it to the ranch in time for a midnight snack.*

He pointed at a green exit sign. "I'm gonna get off here. Help me look for a place to stop."

"Don't do that on my account," she managed to say, her tone brittle. As much as she appreciated that he'd come over to help with packing and dinner last night, it was a tad humiliating. On top of having to cancel paying jobs this weekend, she couldn't accomplish basic tasks? Not being able to ride for ten minutes without needing to scout out another restroom intensified her mounting frustration.

"Oh, this isn't for you, it's for me. Old junior rodeo injury." He tapped his side. "My hip jams sometimes. Need to stretch my legs."

The corner of her mouth quirked. "You expect me to believe that load of horse manure?"

He grinned, unabashed. "Hey, I'm trying to salvage your pride here. The least you could do is play along."

When he winked at her from beneath the brim of his black cowboy hat, she couldn't help but laugh.

They changed lanes to make their way toward the exit ramp, winding up behind a huge truck that said Lanagan Brothers across its back doors. "Speaking of brothers," Garrett said, "what did yours say about our little road trip?"

She bit her lip.

"You *did* tell them? We'll be gone three days, and I know you wouldn't want them to worry."

"I was planning to call them from the road," she said brightly. "At a safe distance. Like maybe your parents' driveway."

He smirked. "That explains why I didn't find Justin at your front door this morning. I half expected to see one of them waiting with a duffel bag and the announcement that he was tagging along."

"With time, I think you could all become friends." Her words came out with less conviction than she'd hoped.

"Don't sweat it. Everyone's families come with their own peculiar baggage. Mine especially."

She saw the way his fingers tightened on the steering wheel, and her heart ached for him. One of the reasons she'd agreed to this trip was because she knew he'd been avoiding his mother in Cielo Peak. Arden didn't want to provide an excuse for him to stay away from home, away from his problems. Still, the thought of his parents made her uneasy. She'd been astonished that Garrett was bringing her to meet the Frosts without first warning them that she was carrying their grandchild. She hoped this wasn't, on a subconscious level, petty retribution—him springing this shock on his mother after she'd dropped her own bombshell. *Bound to be the most awkward introductions in the history of Colorado.*

When she'd tried to suggest giving them a heads-up would allow his parents more time to adjust, he'd become prickly, so Arden had dropped the subject, aware that he already had ample reason to be irate with her. Other than that, he'd been the perfect travel companion, thoughtful and funny with decent taste in road-trip music.

"Aha!" Garrett indicated a billboard for a family-owned place that was both a diner and a country store.

They followed the directions and reached a building that looked like an adorable stone cottage on steroids. There were two separate entrances at either end. Garrett parked near the door leading into the shop.

He unbuckled his seat belt. "Want a souvenir for your collection?"

This had been his running gag for the day. The first time they'd stopped, she'd remarked that she hated to use an establishment's restroom without buying something. So he'd jokingly purchased her a shot glass while he waited. At the following two places, he'd presented her with a postcard and the gaudiest ink pen she'd ever seen in her life, closer to the size of a rolling pin. It was a feathered monstrosity that played bird calls when you pressed buttons on the barrel.

He'd looked inordinately proud. "I've outdone myself. How am I going to top this?"

She'd pursed her lips to keep from giggling. "You are only allowed to buy me bottled water for the rest of this trip, you lunatic."

As they strolled up the sidewalk, she reminded him firmly, "Just water. Got it?"

He tipped his hat at her. "Yes, ma'am."

They stepped inside, and a blonde woman behind the cash register called out a friendly hello. Arden headed for the sign that said restroom, smiling inwardly when she heard Garrett ask the blonde to point him in the direction of the bottled water. A few minutes later, Arden reemerged and discovered that the blonde had come around the counter, abandoning her post to stand much closer to Garrett. She was practically draped across him as she laughed at something he said.

To be fair, Arden assumed the woman needed his proximity for body heat. After all, the tiny little thing was wearing a cropped sweater with low-slung skinny jeans. Exposing so much midriff, she must be chilly. Beneath the fluorescent lights, a dark orange jewel winked in her navel. A pierced belly button and a flat stomach. Arden sighed, recalling her own reflection in the ladies' room mirror. She felt like a bloated, overripe tomato in the bulky coat she wore—its bright red color had been so appealing in the store, but now...

Garrett suddenly turned, as if sensing her presence. "There you are. I got the water. Anything else you need?"

Only to get out of here. She shook her head. "Ready when you are."

The blonde pursed her lips in a pout, laying her hand on Garrett's arm. "Leaving so soon? You should stay and have some lunch at the diner. The bison burger is my favorite, but we also have a wonderful Denver omelet and green chili."

"Actually, we already have lunch plans," Arden said, sidling closer to Garrett. Since she'd made a beeline for the restroom when they walked in, it was probable the blonde hadn't gotten a good look at her yet. Once the cashier realized Arden was pregnant, would she assume Arden and Garrett were a couple?

Whether the woman noticed her or not, she didn't put any space between her and Garrett. She managed to reach for the business card holder on the counter without ever taking her eyes on him. "Next time you come through this way, give me a call. Maybe we can have that lunch together."

He didn't take the card. "Appreciate the offer, ma'am, but I'm not in these parts often."

His refusal should have mollified Arden, but her temper was still smoldering when they got back into the truck. Not that she had any claim on Garrett, or cared who he found attractive. But wasn't there a code between females, an inherent rule that you didn't flirt with another woman's guy right in front of her? Garrett wasn't hers, of course, but the blonde hadn't known that. The rational conclusion, after seeing them together, was—

"I got you something to go with the water." Garrett rustled the brown paper bag in his hand, and she wondered what he would pull out of it. Snow globe? A decorative plate featuring the Sangre de Cristo Mountains?

A squeak of excitement escaped her when she saw the familiar gold wrapping. "Are those what I think they are?" Manners temporarily forgotten, she lunged for the package. "They're my favorite! How did you know?" These particular caramel-filled, individually wrapped chocolate medallions weren't always easy to find. She never would have thought to look in a kitschy little market on the side of a low-trafficked road.

He grinned, clearly pleased with himself. "There were some in the candy dish on the coffee table at your house. I recognized the logo when I saw it again in the store."

"Oh, these are the *best!* I could kiss y—" She broke off abruptly, then wished she hadn't. It was just a stupid expression. By stopping midsentence, she gave the words more weight than she should have had. "Thank you."

"You're welcome." But he didn't start the truck. He was watching her, and she could feel the heat in his gaze.

A shiver of awareness ran through her. For the first time, Arden wondered if she'd gotten in over her head when she'd agreed to this trip.

In spite of the circumstances under which he'd left, driving through the wrought-iron archway of the Double F filled Garrett with the same sense of joyous homecoming it always had. He loved his home, these sprawling ranges of short-grass and sand-sage prairie where generations of Frosts had made their living. His grandparents now resided in an assisted-living home in the nearby town, but Brandon brought them here at least one weekend a month for Sunday supper. During some visits they all fished at the spring-fed lake, other times they simply played cards on the wraparound porch that circled the two-story brick house.

Garrett lived farther back in a modest one-story. He

experienced a wave of excitement mixed with nerves as he imagined showing Arden his place. When he'd left, he certainly hadn't been expecting to bring someone back with him. Would she like his house? Would she be cataloguing all the potential dangers to a baby? The good news was he didn't have stairs. But when he considered all the other possible hazards, it made his head spin.

"I'll buy outlet covers the next time I go to town," he announced. "That's a standard part of baby-proofing, right? I'm completely open to making whatever changes necessary. Just let me know what needs to be done."

She was quiet, the silence heavy around them. Was she thinking about all she still needed to do to prepare? He knew she'd hoped to take care of the baby registry this weekend and that she was worried about how fast time was flying. Or was her pensiveness caused by the idea of the baby being here with him and, by default, not with her?

His parents' house was directly in front of them. "Do you want to stop here, or would you rather come back after we've had a chance to drop off our bags at my place and freshen up?"

"We've already made them wait long enough. Let's get out here." But her tone was bleakly unenthusiastic as she shrugged back into her coat.

Garrett had a sudden paralyzing moment of doubt over his decision to bring her. Was it too stressful, meeting his parents like this? What kind of selfish idiot subjected a pregnant woman with dangerously high blood pressure to a nerve-wracking situation? "We don't have to do this, sweetheart. We could turn around and—"

But Brandon and Caroline were already hollering their greetings as they hustled down the porch steps. Obviously, someone had been keeping watch for his truck.

Arden's smile was sad, her tone wistful. "They sure are eager to see you."

She was unmistakably missing her own parents. His reservations about this trip evaporated. Even though he and Arden weren't dating, they were still linked by the baby. Given time, his parents, the only grandparents her child would have, could become like Arden's honorary extended family.

They climbed out of the truck just as his parents reached them.

"'Bout time you got your butt back here," Brandon chided with gruff affection. "I'm too old a man to be running this place by myself."

Garrett blew out his breath in a rude noise. "Good thing we have half a dozen employees, then, huh?" He threw his arm around his dad's broad shoulders and hugged him. Looking at him now, with a fresh perspective, Garrett wondered why he'd never noticed there was no resemblance between them. Brandon had brown eyes and sandy-blond hair, though it was liberally streaked with silver under his ubiquitous Stetson. His build was more compact than Garrett's, his features blunter.

If Garrett hadn't inherited his mother's coloring and facial characteristics, would the truth have come out sooner?

He nodded to Caroline, using introductions as a way to put off embracing her. "Dad, Mom, I want you to meet someone very special. This is Arden Cade."

As she lifted her hand in a timid wave, her coat slid, giving them a much clearer look at her figure.

"Oh, sweet mercy," Caroline breathed, her hand flying to her mouth. She impaled Garrett with a gaze full of impatient questions. "N-nice to meet you. I'm Caroline Frost."

Arden shook the woman's hand. "I've heard a lot about you."

Garrett was impressed at Arden's warmth. There'd been no irony in her tone despite all she knew about his mother.

"And you," Arden said, turning to his dad with a broad smile, "must be Brandon Frost. Your son really looks up to you."

Brandon cleared his throat twice, then hugged Arden with almost comic gentleness, as if he were worried she might break. "So, um, how long have you and my son known each other?"

"We met at Hugh's wedding," Garrett said. "About six and a half months ago."

Pink swept across Arden's cheeks, and she shot him a reproving glare. Was she annoyed that he'd told the truth? He glared back. His father was being lied to enough without Garrett further prevaricating.

Brandon glanced between the two of them, then dropped his arm around Arden's shoulders in a protective manner. "It's cold out here today. Let's get you inside, young lady." He steered her toward the house, their heads close together as if they'd known each other for years.

Caroline whistled under her breath. "Wow. He's a

good man, but I'm not sure I've ever seen him take to someone *that* fast."

Garrett had no intention of lagging behind and being forced into conversation with his mom. She'd no doubt have questions and opinions regarding his pregnant guest. It was only on the top step of the porch that he temporarily slowed, his gaze straight ahead, his voice low.

"Do you know if Will…has his condition changed?"

"No," Caroline said from behind him. "Dialysis and prayers are still the status quo."

He acknowledged her words with a curt nod and stepped inside the house, trying not to feel as though the life he'd known there had been an illusion.

ARDEN HAD EXPECTED a polite interrogation, but Brandon wasn't asking her any questions. Was he waiting until they were seated at the lunch table, or until he'd had a chance to discuss the facts with his son first? At some point, Brandon or Caroline would ask Arden how far along she was or when she was due and they'd be able to piece together that Arden had jumped into bed with him immediately after meeting him. Would they mentally brand her a shameless hussy? Would they assume it was typical behavior of hers, sleeping with men she didn't know? Might they even worry she was some kind of gold digger who'd schemed to entrap a cattle baron?

Oblivious to her inner monologue, Brandon Frost seemed content to squire her through the long hallway leading to the dining room. The walls were covered with pictures of Garrett through the years. The Frosts obviously doted on their son.

Her mood brightened when she spotted an eight-by-ten of Garrett in elementary school, grinning at the camera with that mischievous smile Arden knew. In the photo, the smile revealed that his two top front teeth were missing. "That is so cute! He's adorable." Since she had no idea whether she was carrying a boy or girl, she rarely imagined what her child might look like. But suddenly she had a visual. Oh, how she'd love to have a miniature version of this face glowing up at her as he told her about his day.

"Adorable?" Garrett echoed from down the hall. "Hale, hearty cowboys such as myself are not *adorable*."

She tapped the frame. "This picture says otherwise. I may have to start calling you cutie-pie."

"You may also have to walk back to Cielo Peak," he responded.

Brandon clucked his tongue. "No talk of leaving yet! You two just got here." He gave Arden a knowing smile. "When he took off last week, with very little explanation, I wondered what was so important in Cielo Peak. Guess now we know. Reckon you've been meeting him on those periodic weekend trips he takes?"

"Actually, no," Garrett said. "There's nothing romantic between me and Arden."

Her face flamed. She'd entertained the far-fetched notion that springing her on his parents like this was minor revenge for his mother's affair. It was slowly dawning on Arden that she might have had the right idea but the wrong target. At the moment, it seemed an awful lot like a vindictive response to her hiding the pregnancy.

She wasn't the only person who'd gone red in the face. Brandon's expression had also grown ruddier. "Oh. But I thought…" His gaze, full of confusion, fell to her stomach.

"It's your son's baby," she confirmed, raising her chin imperiously. Irritation with Garrett bolstered her confidence. "Perhaps the more accurate statement would have been there's nothing romantic between us now." Or ever again. She blasted Garrett with a fulminating glare, then—proud of how serene she sounded—told Caroline, "Something smells wonderful."

"She made Garrett's favorite," Brandon said.

Seeming eager to move on and dispel the tension, he led them into the dining room. A dark cherry oval table had been set with plates and silverware. Goblets of ice waited to be filled with beverages, and the sweet buttery aroma of cornbread wafted from the woven basket at the center of the table.

"I'll get the sweet tea while Caro checks on the casserole," Brandon said pointedly. He might as well have held up a sign declaring that he was giving Garrett and Arden a moment alone.

She wasted no time. Maybe some women employed the silent treatment, but she'd been raised by two brothers who'd taught her how to stand up for herself and, when the occasion called for it, swear like a sailor. "You ass," she hissed. "Is this why you didn't want to tell them ahead of time that I'm pregnant? Because you thought it would be more fun to make everyone uncomfortable and paint me as some kind of skank with loose morals?"

"Fun?" he echoed in an incredulous whisper. "Explaining a baby I knew nothing about until this week to a mother I can barely look in the eye and a father who's no relation to me? Yeah. Good times, Arden. Fine, maybe I could have used a smoother approach—"

She snorted.

"—but I will not lie to them about us. They deserve better. And so do you," he said unexpectedly. "I could mislead them about our relationship, but, trust me, you don't want that. Feeling like someone's secret, waiting for the other shoe to drop…"

Her anger slipped a notch. Garrett had been wonderful at the doctor's yesterday and for most of today. She'd known this homecoming would be challenging for him. Maybe it shouldn't have caught her off-guard that his terse explanations had been so graceless.

"And nobody who spent as much as thirty seconds with you could think you're a skank," he said earnestly. "I meant what I said to my parents. You're special. My dad never takes to people that quickly."

Bemused, she took her seat at the table while Brandon filled everyone's glass with tea. Sometimes there was such tenderness in Garrett's tone, yet other times, contempt flashed in his eyes. She recalled what he'd told her after the dinner with her brothers, that he didn't want to be a bitter, angry man. She could see him wrestling with the ways he'd been wronged. She hated that she'd contributed to that inner struggle.

Caroline returned with some kind of cheesy chicken casserole that made Arden's mouth water. The two women sat across from each other, while Garrett and his father sat on either end. Both men had removed their hats for the meal and set them on a side table.

Settling her napkin in her lap, Caroline looked at Arden. "I probably should have thought to ask before now—you don't have any food allergies, do you? Or foods you can't tolerate during pregnancy?"

"I'm avoiding shellfish and a few other items for the time being, but mostly, I can eat everything. And this looks delicious."

"Thank you." Caroline ladled a portion of the casserole onto her husband's plate and passed it back to him. "There are so many people in our church now with dairy or nut or gluten allergies. I never know what to bring to potluck anymore."

"I feel terrible for the Sunday school teacher, Bess Wilder," Brandon said. "Poor woman's allergic to chocolate. She's never once been able to eat Caro's award-winning brownies. Our friend Will has it worse. Diabetic." His expression grew shadowed. "'Course, now he has more to worry about than just missing out on dessert."

Arden noticed that Garrett had gone stock-still, his entire body rigid. And Caroline's gaze darted between her husband and son—she looked like a trapped animal that didn't know where to run. Garrett had said his biological father was diabetic and a family friend. Her heart squeezed in sympathy. It couldn't be easy to bite back the truth whenever Will's name was mentioned.

She wished she was sitting closer to Garrett so she could hold his hand or rub his shoulder. A silly impulse, perhaps, since patting his shoulder would do nothing to improve his circumstances, but she wanted to lend him strength. The way he had at her doctor's appointment yesterday.

Arden couldn't help stealing glances at Garrett throughout the meal. He'd barely eaten a bite, even though the recipe was supposedly one of his childhood favorites. Brandon ate almost absently, spending most of his time studying his wife, a concerned frown creasing his brow.

It seemed up to the women to make conversation, and Arden wasn't surprised when the first question came.

Caroline set her fork down. "So, the two of you met at Hugh's wedding? Are you a friend of—what's his wife's name?" She glanced toward Garrett, who acted as if he hadn't heard the question.

"Darcy," Arden related.

Brandon chuckled. "Freckled Hugh Connor, the kid who used to squeal in terror if his folks tried to make him ride a pony at the fair. Can't quite picture him as a married man."

"Well, he's grown now." Ostensibly, Caroline's reply was for her husband, but her gaze was locked rather desperately on Garrett. "His pony phobia was *years* ago. The past isn't always relevant to the present. I'm sure he's a much different person." Her every sentence and gesture seemed an attempt to reach out to her wounded son, who continued to silently stonewall her. It was painful to watch.

Arden wondered what the future held for her and her own unborn child. Would she ever do anything her son or daughter couldn't pardon? That would cut a mother to the quick. "I wasn't actually there as a guest," she told Caroline. "I was the photographer."

"Photographer, huh?" Brandon asked. "That an interesting line of work?"

"Some days, it's more interesting than I'd like. I learned early on that any portrait sessions including children or animals tend to be unpredictable."

"And do you like working with children?" Caroline asked. Her voice was tinged with sadness. Because of the current strain between herself and her now-grown child?

Arden squirmed in her chair, trying not to dwell on her tortuous afternoon with the Tucker twins. "I love it." *Mostly.*

"If you don't mind my asking, will this be your first child?"

"Yes, ma'am."

"*Our* first child," Garrett said unexpectedly. "I should have figured out sooner a better way to tell you that I'm going to be a father. To be honest, I'm…still adjusting to the idea myself."

"Well, becoming a father is momentous. And becoming a grandpappy?" Brandon looked delighted at the prospect. "Hell, Caro, we're getting old."

"Speak for yourself." She sent him a mock scowl, and he grinned back at her. Despite today's undercurrents of tension, it was evident the two of them were crazy about each other.

"How about your folks?" Brandon asked Arden. "Are they excited to have a baby on the way? Do they have grandchildren already?"

Her eyes burned with emotion. "My mother died when I was five, and my father followed her into heaven a few years later."

"Oh, you poor dear." Caroline's tone was distraught. "You're all alone, then?"

"Not completely. I have two older brothers. I'm sure they'll be good uncles." Assuming Colin was around. His growing restlessness scared her. What if he jumped on that damn motorcycle and disappeared, convinced his siblings were better off without his gloom and damaged psyche?

"We'll love the baby enough for two sets of grandparents!" Caroline vowed.

"We plan to register for baby stuff soon," Garrett said, "so you'll have opportunities to start spoiling your grandchild even before he—or she—gets here."

"You don't know the gender?" Caroline asked. "How soon can they tell that?"

"I wanted to wait until the baby's born to find out," Arden said. "I don't care if it's a girl or boy, as long as the little peanut's healthy."

Brandon nodded. "I'm proud to have a son to carry on the ranch and the family name, but I would have loved a daughter, too." He gave Arden a smile so welcoming that her throat constricted. For a split second, she felt a wave of utter belonging.

She was confident these two people would love her child, and she wanted that for the baby. The chance for grandparents was a gift she wouldn't have been able to offer as a single mom. But it hurt, the Frosts' acceptance of her. It was a cruel tease, showing her something she hadn't had in a long time but couldn't keep.

Or was she, as Layla would say, borrowing trouble? Life was short. Perhaps she should try to appreciate the blessing of this day and take the future as it came.

"Caroline, can I help you with the dishes?" she offered, wanting to repay their hospitality.

"Absolutely not!" Garrett objected. "There were multiple reasons I brought Arden home with me this weekend, but a major one was to keep an eye on her and make sure she doesn't overexert herself. Dr. Mehta says her blood pressure is too high. He didn't go so far as putting her on strict bed rest, but she's supposed to stay off her feet."

Brandon studied her, seeming to sense her frustration. "Don't you fret. Maybe I can't give you the standard walking tour of the ranch, but we can take the Gator."

She stared at him blankly.

"All-terrain vehicle," Garrett clarified. "We've got several kinds of transportation on the ranch, from tractor to snowmobile, but my favorite mode has always been horseback. I'm getting up early tomorrow to ride the perimeter and check fencing. See if there are any repairs we need to make before the serious winter weather rolls in."

"I've never been riding," she said. "I think I sat on a horse to get my picture taken at a birthday party when I was little, but that's about it." Justin and Colin had loved skiing and snowboarding. They'd been more eager to get her on the slopes than in a saddle.

"After the baby comes, maybe we—" Garrett stopped, catching himself. Whatever the future held, Arden doubted his girlfriends down the road would be thrilled about him spending recreational time with his former one-night stand. Even if—especially if—she was the mother of his child.

He recovered admirably, making it look as if he'd interrupted himself to say something else. "Hey, Dad gave me an idea. You wanted to register for baby gifts, but the doc said to stay off your feet. Don't most big stores have those motorized carts now? You can drive from one end of the store to the other."

She knew he meant well, but the suggestion highlighted the grating powerlessness she'd felt ever since the doctor said she had to cancel her jobs this weekend. It was mortifying to feel helpless, prohibited from simple tasks like dishes and shopping. Plus, though she was reluctant to admit to such pettiness, motoring around on one of those carts would chafe her ego. She was a young, comparatively athletic woman in the prime of her life! It had been bad enough standing next to Garrett while that crop-topped blonde with the bejeweled belly button flirted with him. She could just imagine following him around like some giant parade float while lissome salesgirls fawned over him and offered their assistance.

"Another option," Caroline said, "is to register on-line. We like not living in a city, clogged with traffic and malls, but I have to admit, being able to use the internet for shopping makes it a lot easier."

"Oh, yeah," Brandon grumbled good-naturedly. "She can whip out a credit card and buy anything her heart desires at any hour of the day. Hurray."

"So I suppose you want me to cancel those gifts I ordered for your birthday in November?" Caroline teased. She swung back to Arden. "Speaking of November, do you have plans for Thanksgiving, dear?"

"Only if you count having a baby," Arden said, trying not to gulp. She couldn't wait to meet her child, but thinking about the birth process was still daunting. She kept trying to skip over that part in her mind and look forward to Christmas. Last year had been the first holiday season since Natalie's and Danny's deaths; Arden hadn't even dredged up the energy to put up a tree. She and Justin had exchanged gifts and toasted each other with heavily spiked eggnog. Colin had insisted on being alone. This year, she planned to celebrate the biggest gift of her life.

"I've read all the recommended books," Arden said, "and I'm signed up for classes through the hospital, but I'm a nervous wreck."

"I understand completely," Caroline admitted. "The whole time I was carrying Garrett, I was convinced something would go wrong again."

"Again?" Arden asked.

"Oh! I...is that what I said?" Visibly shaken, Caroline bolted from her chair and carried her plate to the kitchen.

Brandon excused himself, gathering up more dishes and leaving to check on his wife.

Arden glanced at Garrett, who seemed confused. Had Caroline been pregnant before she had him? "Do you know what that was about?" she asked softly.

He shrugged. "Not a clue."

"Maybe we should give them some space," she suggested.

When Caroline returned a few minutes later to ask if anyone had room for dessert, Arden shook her head. "Actually, I'm more tired than hungry. I was just asking Garrett if we could take our stuff to his house. I may stretch out and take a nap."

"Of course. You two just come back when you're ready this evening. We'll have dinner and maybe play some card games." Her smile lacked its previous luster, but she was obviously trying to project cheer. "Have you ever played pinochle, dear? Brandon and I are formidable. Regional champs."

"Never tried it, but good to know I'll be learning from the best," Arden said.

"Thank you for lunch, Mom." But Garrett didn't so much address Caroline as the pale blue wall over her left shoulder.

As they left, Arden snuck one last glimpse at Mrs. Frost, who stood alone in the center of the dining room, shoulders slumped in dejection. She was staring down, so Arden didn't get a look at her expression, but her body language was clear. She was a woman with a broken heart.

"MY HOUSE ISN'T very big." Garrett pulled their bags from the truck, feeling foolish for having stated the obvious. His house had always been more than adequate, focused on the exact luxuries he wanted and none of the unnecessary extras his mother had given up suggesting—like vases or "curio cabinets." What the hell was a curio? "It's kind of like yours, actually. So the peanut should feel right at home."

In his peripheral vision, he saw Arden flinch.

"Does it bother you, when I talk about having the baby with me? I'm not trying to separate you from Peanut, you know. I just want to be a father." His throat tightened. "Do you know how many milestones I'll miss? It's unlikely I'll be there for the first step or the first word. At best, they'll probably be blurry videos I get to see weeks later on your phone." If she'd had her way, he wouldn't have even experienced those.

"Garrett…"

There wasn't a damn thing she could say to change the circumstances or take back what she'd done. Shaking his head, he strode toward the house.

He unlocked the door and held it open for her, letting her step into the living room first.

The look she gave him over her shoulder was wry. "So this place is like mine, huh?"

Granted, she didn't own a big-screen television or a leather sectional sofa, but the analogy wasn't completely off-base. "Maybe without some of the homier details," he admitted.

On the mantel he had a framed picture of himself with his parents and grandparents and a much smaller photo of his favorite horse. They were the only photographs displayed anywhere in his home. He suddenly felt self-conscious about that, given Arden's profession. But mountains and spectacular sunsets and countless stars winking down at his porch were part of his daily existence. Why miniaturize them for capture in insignificant pewter frames when he could experience them firsthand?

"The good news is, I have plenty of room for baby paraphernalia," he joked.

The furniture was sparse, but that helped keep the modest-size house uncluttered. His philosophy was that he didn't need much, so for the belongings he *did* purchase, why not buy the best? He'd spent most of his budget on the high-end sectional sofa but skipped over a kitchen table. Between bar stools at the counter, fold-ing TV trays and meals at the main house, he figured he was covered. Did Arden see an indulgent bachelor pad? He had to admit, his style of living wasn't necessarily compatible with having an infant or toddler in the house.

He scratched his jaw. "Guess I need to change more than just the outlet covers, huh?"

She hesitated as if there were something she wanted to say but thought better of it.

"Arden?"

"I actually am tired. Is there a place I can lay down for a while?"

"Right this way." He took her to the master suite. Something potent jolted through him. He'd always been sexually drawn to Arden, but having her here by his bed made the desire more primal. More possessive.

She took in her surroundings. "This isn't a guest room."

"Don't have one anymore. This house was over seventy years old. I did a complete remodel, including knocking out the wall between two small bedrooms. Figured less was more. Literally. You'll sleep in here, I've got the living room. The middle section of the sofa pulls out into a surprisingly comfortable double bed. Bathroom's right this way."

"Whoa." She gaped at the spacious tub. Its hot-water jets were perfect for easing sore muscles after days of sunup to sundown labor. "That's big enough for two people, easily."

The mental image was vivid and instantaneous. He tried not to groan at the thought of slicking soap over her dewy skin. The morning they'd woken up together in that Cielo Peak hotel, he'd hoped she'd join him in the shower. Instead, she'd stolen away without a backward glance.

He cleared his throat. "Unless you need anything else, I'm headed to the barn to help my dad." Putting much-needed space between himself and his alluring houseguest. "I've got my cell phone with me."

Although Garrett truly loved the ranch, he didn't think he'd ever been this eager to tackle menial chores. There was a specific calm that came with the familiar tasks—cowboy Zen his dad had called it once.

He found Brandon starting the tractor.

"About to haul hay," the older man called. "Wanna lend a hand?"

"Sure." Garrett stepped up onto the platform step and held on. The tractor chugged toward the round bales they would use to stock feeders. Sometimes the two men rode in companionable silence. Garrett knew today would not be one of those days.

Brandon came out swinging, raising his voice to be heard over the engine. "You gonna do the right thing and marry that purty gal?"

"Dad, I told you, it's not like that between us. We aren't dating." Relationships required trust. These days, Garrett was feeling pretty cynical about the institution of marriage in general. But that wasn't something he could discuss.

"I don't know what you mean by *dating,* but whatever you did was enough to get her pregnant." Brandon made a derisive noise. "You were brought up in a good home, with parents who loved each other. Didn't think you were one of those men with dumb-ass priorities, the ones too afraid to grow up and settle down."

"That's not it at all," Garrett said, defending himself. "And you're making an awfully big assumption that even if I asked her, she'd say yes. Arden…has been through a lot. She told you she lost her parents. About a year ago, she also lost her best friend and young nephew in a car crash. She's…in a delicate place emotionally, picking up the pieces."

A wholly unexpected stab of guilt twisted Garrett's insides. Whether he'd known it or not, Arden *had* been emotionally vulnerable the night he'd slept with her. He hadn't meant to take advantage of her loss. All he'd known was that the beautiful stranger made his blood boil with need. Hell, she still did.

Arden had said she wanted them to be friends. Did she have any feelings for him beyond that? She'd kissed him at her house but had been quick to blame pregnancy hormones. Had she been trying to tell them that her body might want him, but, aside from the ungoverned chemical reaction, she wasn't interested?

"Caught your momma and me off-guard," Brandon chided, "springing Arden on us like that. Don't get me wrong. We're happy to meet her. She seems like good people. But your momma… Long before we had you, there were miscarriages. Caro's tough enough to hold her own against a coyote or a snake, but she wasn't emotionally prepared to spend the afternoon with a pregnant woman."

Garrett didn't know what to say. "How come neither of you mentioned any of this before?"

His dad shrugged. "Never saw the need. Why dredge up old pain when it's in the past?"

They reached the bales and began the process of lifting them for transportation to the feeders. For now, conversation was over. But his dad's words kept replaying through Garrett's mind. Did Brandon truly believe it was better for the past to lay undisturbed? Caroline Frost insisted that telling her husband about her long-ago indiscretion would cause him pointless grief, that it was a fleeting mistake with no consequence on the present.

Except that wasn't true. Garrett was the consequence. Brandon always talked about the Double F as if it were the family legacy. But right now it felt as if their legacy was comprised of unintentional pregnancies and women who kept secrets.

Striving to push aside the doubt and questions—at least for one afternoon—Garrett threw himself into the familiar rhythm of feeding the cows. He envied the herd their simple existence. As far as his own life was concerned, it felt as if no decision would ever be simple again.

Chapter Nine

Arden suppressed a yawn, staring out the window at hundreds of twinkling stars. "I may have to spend the night in the truck. I'm too stuffed to move. Not that I'm complaining."

"I have to say, my mother went all out. She must really like you."

Was he really that blind? *Arden* wasn't the one Caroline was trying so hard to win over. "I would've said it was more a case of slaughtering the fatted calf to welcome home the prodigal son. In this case, literally." The Frosts' freezer was full of prime beef they themselves had raised. Had it been strange for him as a boy, eating a steak that might have had a name only a few months ago?

"I'm not that *prodigal*. I was only gone for a week."

"Nonetheless, she's happy to have you home. Happy and scared. She's afraid you won't forgive her."

"You think I *want* to be angry with her? I didn't ask for any of this. Waffling between all these emotions sucks. It's confusing. And exhausting." As they walked toward the house, a motion-sensor light flooded the yard.

She took the opportunity to steal a better look at his

expression. Did he classify her in the "any of this" he hadn't asked for, one of the factors currently screwing up his life? She would never, ever wish away the baby, but for the first time, it occurred to her to wonder what would have happened if she hadn't been pregnant when she'd encountered Garrett in the grocery store. Would they have met for a drink, maybe? Reexplored their physical connection? Would there have been a chance for them to develop something more?

"I know what you mean about the emotional exhaustion," she said. "When Natalie and Danny died, I was livid. But maintaining that level of outrage over the unfairness of it all left me depleted. Listless. It was a long, slow climb up out of that pit." Her night with Garrett had been a major catalyst in that process. She only wished there was more she could do to help him with his own personal crisis.

Inside, he asked, "Ready to turn in?"

"No. I slept too long this afternoon," she said ruefully. His bed was impossibly comfortable. "But if you're tired, I can read or something."

He didn't answer at first, and she wondered what he was thinking. Would he prefer the solitude of his own company? Or was he as reluctant to say good-night as she was? "How about we look into that online registry idea?" he suggested finally. "My computer's in the bedroom."

Fifteen minutes later, as Arden wiggled her bare toes and sipped from a steaming mug of generously honeyed chamomile tea, she decided that Caroline Frost was a genius for having thought of this. Arden had changed into a pair of pajamas, and Garrett was stretched out next to her in a pair of plaid flannel pants and a well-worn charcoal T-shirt, his muscles delineated beneath the thin cotton. This was *so* much better than rolling alongside him at a retail warehouse like his fat cyborg friend.

They hadn't gotten to any of the fun stuff yet—the actual scrolling through products and clicking on anything and everything that looked useful. Garrett was still inputting their basic information, listing her as the main contact and her address for shipping. She thought about what he'd said earlier, that his wanting to spend time with the baby was nonmalicious and that she was welcome to spend time here, too. After tonight, she could almost imagine doing so. Caroline and Brandon had entertained her with stories of Garrett's childhood and ranch life; they'd coaxed her to talk about herself and said her brothers sounded like absolute princes— which had earned a sarcastic guffaw from Garrett.

She nudged his ankle with her foot. "You have a strange surname."

"Frost? That's not weird."

"It is for a family this warm. Thank you for bringing me here. Your parents are wonderful people. *You're* wonderful." When the time came that her child was spending weekends and holidays and summers here without her, she would always know that the kid was in good hands.

But now was not the time for such bittersweet thoughts. She wanted to distract herself with cute one-sies and colorful board books, not dwell on the challenges to come. "Maybe I should've typed," she mocked him. "Even with swollen hands, I could go faster than you."

"Not my fault," he grumbled, moving his fingers in an inefficient, hunt-and-peck fashion. "Your pajamas are distracting me."

She blinked. "My pajamas?"

"They're sexy."

The sky-blue drawstring shorts printed with bright yellow rubber duckies and the voluminous matching top? "Are you on crack?" A walking lingerie ad, she was not.

"Rubber ducks are for the bathtub," he said, as though this made something resembling sense. "Ever since what you said earlier…I might have pictured you in the tub once or twice."

A sweet, piercing heat flooded her. "Oh." He'd pictured her there? She was surprised by the intensity in his tone, how much he wanted her. True, they'd had incredible sex together, but that had been months ago. Before she'd damaged his trust. Before her body had morphed to its current shape. "Did you, um, picture yourself in the tub with me?"

He jerked his head up, looking startled by the question. Then he set the laptop on the comforter and leaned very close. "Yes." His breath fanned over her skin. "Would you like to hear the details?"

"I… No, I…" Frankly, she'd rather have a demonstration. But no matter how loudly the reckless words echoed in her head, she couldn't bring herself to voice them.

"I understand." He picked up the laptop again as if nothing had happened. She tried not to hate him for that.

Her breathing was shallow, her palms were clammy, her nipples were hard points. He resumed the uneven staccato of his typing.

Arden gulped her tea as if it were a miracle cure for lust, and immediately cursed.

"Whoa. Some language." Garrett looked impressed at her imaginative vulgarity.

"I was raised by older brothers," she said by way of explanation. But since she'd burned her tongue, it came out as *I wath raithed by older brotherth.* Very sexy. No wonder a gorgeous cowboy who could probably have his pick of any woman in the state spent time fantasizing about her. *Sheesh.*

"Okay, all done filling out the online form," Garrett declared. "Do you have a checklist of everything we need?"

"At home. I didn't pack it this weekend. But we can get started and always add items in later." She scooted closer so she could see the screen better and directed him to consumer reviews and safety reports on the car seats that interested her the most. It took them over forty minutes of research and debate to decide on a seat, a crib and a high chair.

He hesitated, his hand hovering over the mouse. "Should we register for two cribs?"

It was a fair question, and she tried not to balk. "How about this? We register for a playpen. It's basically a portable crib that you can fold up and throw in the back of the truck. Not only would it work well here at your place, you could easily schlep it over to your parents' for a few hours in case you wanted to visit with them or they offered to babysit."

After a number of big items had been selected, they began surfing the site just for fun. "Why are there no baby cowboy hats?" Garrett demanded. "That's a travesty!"

She had a sudden mental image of a little boy with Garrett's shimmering gray eyes, a too-big cowboy hat dipping comically low over his forehead.

"Oh, dear Lord." His befuddled tone snapped her out of her reverie. "Now I've seen everything."

"What is it?"

"Baby Booty Balm. Then there's another brand called Butt Spackle. Can't these people just call it diaper rash ointment? Leave the poor kids some dignity."

A succession of memories drifted through her mind—mental snapshots of Danny dressed like a bunny at Easter when he'd only been four months old, him covered in mud after he'd discovered a puddle in the yard, and streaking bare-assed through a dinner party once when he'd emphatically decided his father was *not* going to change his diaper.

"Hate to burst your bubble," she said, "but I'm not sure infancy and toddlerhood come with a lot of *dignity*."

"You never know," he quipped. "Our kid could be special."

Of that, she had no doubt. They made a few more selections, and she realized that the soothing chamomile had done its job. A peaceful lassitude was seeping through her bones. With Garrett next to her, making jokes about their son or daughter, she felt more tranquil and lighthearted than she had in weeks. Not wanting the moment to end, she tried to smother her yawn, but he noticed.

"Why don't we shut this off for now?" He clicked on an icon to bookmark the page, and she noticed some of the other sites in the "favorites" library. Most of them were about kidney transplants and living donors.

"Interesting reading," she remarked. She didn't want to pry, but she hoped that by giving him an opening, he'd know she was available to listen.

"Kidneys are among the most common organ transplants," he said. "And, if I read this one article right, doctors don't actually remove the bad kidney to replace it. They leave it in there and do some kind of…I don't know, arterial rerouting? Like when someone used to hack their neighbor's cable. So whenever Will gets a new kidney, he'll be walking around with three of them inside." Garrett frowned. "Three's an awkward number."

"How do you mean?"

"What was your impression of my parents together?" he asked. "As a couple?"

The question surprised her, but it meant a lot to her that he valued her opinion. "From my perspective as an outsider, it looks as if they're crazy about each other. I can't imagine why your mother was ever with someone else, but if she says it ended years ago, I'd believe her."

Garrett jammed a hand through his hair. "You may be right. I mean, I certainly never saw anything when I was younger to make me suspicious. I always thought my parents were devoted to each other, a shining example. I wanted, someday, to find what they had."

Was he angry not just that Caroline had betrayed

her husband but that she'd betrayed Garrett's long-held ideal? Parents were human beings, too. Yes, his mom was flawed, but he was still lucky to have her.

"I think the affair bothers me more because Will Harlow never married," he said. "He'd bring an occasional date to dinner, but I've been racking my brain and can't remember his ever having a serious girlfriend. It makes me wonder if his feelings for my mother were as platonic as she'd like to claim. Did he ever really move on? And does it matter? Even if he's been pining for my mother her entire marriage, is that a reason to deny him a kidney?"

She gave in to the impulse she'd had earlier today to comfort him. Now that they weren't separated by his parents' dining-room table, she put her arm around his midsection and hugged him tightly, resting her head on his chest. He went very still at first, but gradually relaxed, dropping one arm over her shoulders and stroking her hair with his other hand. It was very quiet in the room, only the whir of his laptop providing background noise.

Finally, he broke the silence. "You know I have a consultation scheduled for Monday? That's the first step, followed by several days, up to a week in the hospital. There are physicals, blood tests, psych evaluation…" He sounded overwhelmed.

"I could go with you on Monday," she ventured. "You know, for moral support."

"I'd rather you stay here."

She sat upright. "Are you sure? I know hale-and-hearty cowboys don't admit weakness, but it might be easier for you with someone there."

"Just the opposite. My dad really likes you."

What did that have to do with the price of skis in Denver?

"I already despise that I can't tell him where I'm going," Garrett said hollowly. "Bringing you with me would be like a double betrayal, making you an accessory to the crime."

"Garrett, you may end up saving a man's life—a man your father cares about deeply, by the way. That's hardly a crime." She decided to lighten the mood. "If you end up spending a week in the hospital, can I at least come visit you? Feels like it should be *my* turn to see *you* in one of the embarrassing paper gowns that covers essentially nothing."

He arched an eyebrow. "Here I thought you were being compassionate and supportive, but really you were angling for a look at my ass?"

"Is there a law that a woman can't be nurturing and ogle at the same time?"

He laughed at that, and his smile made her feel as if she'd won the lottery. Their gazes held a fraction of an instant too long. If he asked again whether she wanted to hear the details of his scandalous bathtub daydreams, she'd say yes this time. But he did the sensible thing and held his hand out for her mug.

"I'll wash these out. You can go ahead and brush your teeth, then I'll take my turn."

He gave her plenty of time. She was already in bed with the covers pulled up to her chin when he disappeared into the bathroom. Listening to him gargle mouthwash, she giggled in the dark. She'd lived alone for years and was unaccustomed to sharing the mundane, yet somehow poignant, intimacy of these daily routines.

The bathroom door opened, and Garrett shut off the light. Her eyes needed a moment to readjust—she could hear him but not see him very well. The man had a fantastic voice, rich and addictive like caramel.

"I'm not going to wake you before I saddle up in the morning," he reminded her. "No reason for us both to be up at the crack of dawn. Dad bought me some pastries when he went to town this morning. They'll be out on the counter. There's also a bowl of fruit and plenty of milk and juice. Mom used her spare key to stock the fridge when she heard I was bringing a guest. If you want anything more substantial for breakfast or need company, give Mom a call at the house. Dad bought her a used golf cart a few years ago so she can zip between all the buildings on the property as long as there's no snow on the ground.

"On the other hand," he continued, "if you feel like taking advantage of the opportunity to sleep in, no one would blame you."

"Feels a bit antisocial," she said. "To come all this way to meet your family, then waste half the day in bed." Plus, Brandon still owed her that tour he'd promised. He said the spring-fed lake was particularly beautiful. And he wanted to show her the spot on this very ranch where, thirty-six years ago, he'd proposed to Caroline.

The mattress dipped as Garrett sat next to her. "I think your obstetrician would see it as 'resting,' not 'wasting.' And you're nearly seven months pregnant. Being a little antisocial is your prerogative, okay?"

"Yes, sir." She gave him a jaunty salute.

He sighed. "Why are you mocking me?"

"Force of habit. I grew up with two well-meaning but domineering brothers, so irreverence tends to be my default mode whenever a man tells me something that's for my own good. Not that you were domineering. You're being considerate."

"I try. It hasn't been the easiest thing this week, but I do try. The considerate thing now is to leave you alone so you can sleep."

For a bare second, she thought he might kiss her good-night. Instead, he brushed his thumb over her bottom lip, tracing the sensitive outer edge and doubling back to curve across her top lip. Unable to help herself, she caught the pad of his thumb between her teeth, biting gently. He sucked in his breath, the gasp unnaturally loud in the stillness.

"Arden." That warm caramel voice spilled over her, making her toes curl beneath the sheets. "Even if I wanted to act on the attraction to us, I'm not sure it would be safe for you."

He had a point. In the unlikely event that her blood pressure didn't go back down and Dr. Mehta diagnosed her with preeclampsia, she needed to exercise caution for the duration of her pregnancy. The last thing she wanted to do was risk Peanut's safety.

She felt ashamed. "I'm sorry."

"Don't be." There was so much banked heat in his eyes, she imagined she could see them glowing.

When he headed for the doorway, she succumbed to a moment of weakness and called him back. "Garrett? I know we shouldn't…do anything stimulating. But do you really have to sleep on the couch? We've shared a bed before." She'd slept in his arms over six months ago and hadn't had that kind of closeness with anyone since. Once the baby came, she would have her hands full. It could be a *very* long time before she was serious enough about another man to spend the night with him.

The thought gave her a pang, as if imagining a hypothetical man in Garrett's presence was disloyal. What if…what if she'd already found the man she wanted? *Then you probably shouldn't have elected to cheat him out of the news that he was a father, especially not at the same time he was grappling with the most important woman in his life being a liar and adulteress.* With his scars and trust issues, she almost felt sorry for the next person to date him.

"You want me to stay?" he asked.

"I do." She held her breath.

"Then scoot over, and don't hog the covers."

"Can I put my icy cold feet on you?" she asked sweetly.

"Not unless you want to hear a grown man shriek like a little girl," he said as he slid beneath the sheets.

She rolled to the other side, fluffing her pillow and smiling at his nearness. Then she chuckled. "Figures. He does this every night—it's half the reason I never get decent sleep anymore." She reached for Garrett's hand and placed his palm over her abdomen. "Peanut seems to be gearing up for the 2028 Olympic gymnastics team."

"You called the baby *he,*" Garrett noted. "So you're thinking men's gymnastics, then? Maybe we should have registered for an itty-bitty set of parallel bars."

"It was just a slip of the tongue, not true maternal instinct." The power of suggestion—she'd been visualizing their child as a boy ever since seeing all of Garrett's baby pictures. By the time they'd returned to the main house for dinner tonight, Caroline had pulled out even more albums for Arden to peruse. "We should register for equipment used in both women's and men's gymnastics. Think that site we were on has anything in a miniature vault?"

"They'd better. If they've neglected to stock cowboy hats for newborns *and* essential gym equipment, we may have to take our business elsewhere."

She laughed and, as though responding to the sound, the baby rolled beneath Garrett's hand. "Peanut seems happy," she said. In fact, she herself felt dangerously content.

Snuggled against Garrett now, it was difficult to remember that he was the same person who'd baldly announced to his family earlier today that there was "nothing romantic" between him and Arden. He'd admitted that he was trying extra-hard to be considerate, and he knew from her visit to Dr. Mehta that she shouldn't be exposed to extra stress or conflict. Garrett was humoring the pregnant lady. Just because he'd agreed to her request to stay with her tonight didn't mean anything had changed long-term, that he'd forgiven her.

Still, despite what her logical mind knew to be true, her last absent thought as beckoning oblivion enveloped her was *my family.*

CAROLINE FROST MUST have been standing at her back door, keys in hand, just waiting for Arden's call. Scarcely three minutes after Arden phoned to say she was awake and showered on Sunday morning, Caroline appeared on the porch.

Garrett's front porch wasn't nearly as elaborate as his parents' wraparound veranda, but it was wide enough to accommodate a white swing and two padded chairs. In the spring, it was probably a beautiful place to enjoy the breezy sunshine and watch birds and small animals flit across the pasture.

"Come on inside," Arden welcomed Caroline. "Although, I feel a little foolish issuing the invitation, me being a temporary guest and this house having belonged to your family for generations."

They walked into the living room, where Arden had set out a pot of decaf coffee and pastries on the table.

"I hope you won't think of yourself as a mere guest for long." Caroline settled onto the couch, her expression earnest. "I'll admit, when Garrett told me he was bringing you home this weekend, I had mixed feelings. Nothing personal, dear. I only questioned the timing. But now I'm delighted you're here. I saw the way he looked at you last night. You may be exactly what he needs."

Suddenly Arden wished she'd taken Garrett's guidance about sleeping in this morning. This was the most carefree she'd seen his mother since they arrived, and Arden was about to rob her of her optimistic happiness. "Mrs. Frost—"

The woman harrumphed an unsubtle reminder.

"Sorry. Caroline. I appreciate the compliment, but you know your son and I aren't dating."

"Maybe not at the moment," she said knowingly.

"Maybe not ever. I lied to him. About the baby."

Caroline looked startled. "How do you mean?"

"I never called to tell him he was going to be a father. I'd planned to be a single mom with him none the wiser. And, frankly, I'm not sure he'll ever forgive me. That's not to say he's nurturing a grudge or being unpleasant to me," she was quick to add. "He's been…wonderful, very conscientious about my health and not upsetting me unduly. But there's a barrier between us. I don't know that it will ever completely go away."

"I see." Caroline's hand trembled slightly as she poured two mugs of coffee. "My son's certainly been through a lot. I wish I could promise you that forgiveness will come, but I'm the last person who can say that. Did he tell you that we had…not quite an argument, but a difficult conversation before he left?"

"He told me. About you and Will."

Caroline covered her face with her hands. "What you must think of me!"

"If there's one thing I've learned, we all act rashly at one time or another," Arden said wryly.

"I wanted to explain the whole story to him, my frame of mind at the time—not that it excuses what I did. But he was too damn mad. When he left the ranch, I had no idea how long he'd be gone or what he'd say to Brandon when he returned. I love my husband, Arden. With my heart and soul! I hate myself for what I did to him…but how do I regret having Garrett? My other pregnancies— Oh, but this isn't an appropriate story for a young woman expecting her first child. I don't want to frighten you."

Arden appreciated her thoughtfulness, but Caroline

Frost seemed as if she desperately needed a friendly ear. "I can probably take it. I grew up with the acute awareness that bad things happen. Often without rhyme or reason. One person could live a charmed life and the neighbors next door could lose their grandmother and their dog and have their house burn down all in the same week. I'll try not to let your misfortunes make me paranoid." *Try* being the operative word.

"You're sure?" Caroline licked her lips nervously. "Oh, if you weren't in a family way, I'd pour a healthy dollop of whiskey into both our coffees. Brandon loves this ranch almost as much as he loves me. He grew up here and planned to run it with his two brothers. But one was killed in Vietnam. The other overdosed."

Arden sometimes forgot that tragedy could be just as prevalent in other families as it had been in hers.

"When we got married, he talked all the time about having children. I think he hoped our kids could recreate the dream he lost when his brothers died. I wanted a big family, too," Caroline added with a sad smile. "We hadn't been married a whole year the first time I got pregnant. We were beside ourselves with joy. I lost the baby in the first trimester."

"I'm so sorry." Miscarriages in early pregnancy weren't uncommon, but Arden could see in Caroline's gray eyes—so like her son's—that the memory still haunted her.

"I was devastated, but the doctor assured me it wasn't a sign we'd done anything wrong or couldn't have children. After some time passed, we found out I was expecting again. This time, we didn't tell anyone. I wanted to safely pass that three-month mark first. We never made it that far."

Arden wanted to weep for her. It was easy to imagine the excited young bride and her groom with their dreams of children filling the brick house, playing hide-and-seek in the stables, gallivanting through the pastures, chasing after bunnies and chipmunks.

"Brandon and I never fought while we were dating," Caroline continued, "and we've rarely fought during our marriage. But that was a terrible time for us. Tension was so high. We didn't know—should we try again? Every time we came together as husband and wife, I was torn between half hoping we had conceived and praying we didn't. Then it happened. I was pregnant. I made it all the way to five months." She stopped, hiccupped, tried to catch her breath and stave off the gathering tears.

"You don't have to tell me the rest." Arden felt like hell for encouraging her in the first place. "Really. It's none of my—"

"No, it's okay," Caroline said bravely. "I should have talked this all out with someone a long time ago. You're doing me a favor. That last miscarriage was the worst. The doctors weren't even sure I could have a baby after that. Brandon was enraged, having lost his brothers and repeatedly losing the babies. I was despondent. We barely spoke, neither of us knowing what to say or how to make it better. The only time either of us laughed was when his friend Will joined us for dinner or to play cards. When the doctor told me it was okay to have relations again, Brandon wouldn't touch me.

"Looking back, I think it was fear. He was afraid to

cause me more physical or emotional damage. At the time, it felt like rejection, like I was defective. A piece of livestock he'd sell off because of inherent flaws. We had a horrible argument one night, and he took off."

Arden was so caught up in the tale she forgot to breathe. Even though she'd seen firsthand that the Frosts had overcome their tribulations, it was easy to imagine how scared and alone the woman had felt so many years ago, wondering where her husband had disappeared to and if he would be all right.

"Turns out, he'd holed up in a friend's hunting cabin to think. That's one thing about Frost boys, sometimes they have to go out on their own before they can figure out how to be with the ones they love. This was before the days of cell phones, and I was inconsolable. Bad storms swept into the area the next day, and Will came to look after me. Tornadoes in the area knocked out the power. Will and I lit some candles and made up pallets in the basement, planning to spend the night down there. We talked about Brandon and I cried, afraid he didn't want me anymore. Afraid no man would want me because there was something wrong with me. I…" She broke off on a wail.

When she'd regained a measure of composure, she finished. "It just happened. I know that sounds awful, like I'm not taking any responsibility, but I know I betrayed the man I love." She sounded lost.

Arden handed her one of the napkins from the table, taking another to dab her own eyes.

"The storm was the impetus Brandon needed to come home. As soon as the roads were cleared, he raced back to check on me. Will begged me not to tell Bran-

don what we'd done. He said that with everything Bran
and I had already suffered through, he could never forgive himself if *he* was the straw that broke our marriage.
For years, he wouldn't even come to dinner unless he
had a date with him—a buffer, I guess. After Brandon
and I made up, it took time to coax him back into our
bed. He's a man. He doesn't pay attention to details like
gestational calendars, unless it's calving season, but the
timing didn't line up."

"You knew he wasn't the father," Arden observed.

Caroline nodded. "After the delivery, my doctor did
a procedure to keep me from having more kids. He'd
formed a theory that Bran and I were…incompatible,
medically speaking. We're so blessed to have Garrett.
He's ours in every way that counts. I never would have
told him otherwise if it weren't a matter of life or death."
Her voice was a naked plea, an entreaty for forgiveness
that wasn't Arden's to bestow.

Tears were streaming down both their faces, and
Arden hugged her tightly. They sat like that for a while,
two mothers both understanding the compulsion to do
right for your child amid a minefield of possible wrong
choices.

Caroline straightened. "I've wondered, at times, if
Will had an inkling of the truth, but we didn't speak of
it through my entire pregnancy. As an infant, Garrett
once had to go to the E.R. because his fever was too
high. I realized there may come a day when there was
a medical necessity for Will to intervene. Maybe donat-
ing blood or answering questions about patient history,
whatever. For the sake of my son, I had to talk to Will,
to make sure we were on the same page in case there

was ever a future crisis. I never imagined it would be the other way around, that *he* would be the one needing assistance. Garrett may be too angry to see it right now, to remember it, but Will Harlow is a good man."

"I don't think I can convince Garrett to help Will," Arden said apologetically. "That's a deeply personal decision. But I will seize any opportunity to persuade him to forgive you. For his sake and yours. The time we get to spend with our loved ones can be too brief." If anything happened to Caroline without Garrett first absolving his mother, he would never find peace again.

"Thank you. I'm probably the last person in the world who should give another woman advice, but I'll do it, anyway. As you may discover, Frost men are not always easy to love. But loving them is worth any trials along the way."

Long after Caroline left, her words remained.

Arden could picture them hovering over her like cartoon thought bubbles. *Love Garrett?* That would be total folly.

Feeling suddenly claustrophobic in the house, she wrapped herself in a thick blanket and went out to the porch. Arden had thought herself in love once or twice in the past, but those men were dim memories now. She couldn't imagine a time when Garrett would be a "dim" anything. The larger-than-life cowboy had made more of an impression on her in one week than a past boyfriend had made in a year. The pregnancy muddied the issue. Her feelings for Garrett were tangled up in the love she had for their baby.

If they'd met and dated without this automatic bond between them, would she even be having this mental debate? Was she falling in love, or was she simply overcome with gratitude? Not only had he given her Peanut, but this weekend he'd also given her a sense of home and family she hadn't experienced in a long time.

Much as she adored her brothers, their family was undeniably fractured. She was increasingly frustrated by Justin's glib refusal to let people get close to him, and it felt as though Colin were growing more detached every day.

Motion caught her eye, and she lifted her head, focusing. In the distance, a black horse galloped past, its rider clad in a dark brown duster and a familiar cowboy hat. Even at this distance, her body quivered with yearning, making a mockery of her deliberations.

Whatever she felt for Garrett Frost, it was a hell of a lot more than gratitude.

Chapter Ten

If Arden had thought she was discomfited on the trip to the Double F, with the ordeal of meeting Garrett's parents looming large in her mind, it was nothing compared to the drive back to Cielo Peak on Tuesday morning.

Garrett had returned from his donor consultation the day before more withdrawn than she'd ever seen him. He'd told his father he wasn't feeling well and asked Brandon to fetch Arden to the main house for dinner. At bedtime, he'd gone straight to the fold-out sofa and she hadn't bothered to issue another request that he join her. He obviously craved space, and she refused to be that needy.

What had Caroline said on Sunday? That Frost men had to work through things alone?

Men were fools. Colin was also a believer in solitude over catharsis, but she couldn't see that it was working out for him. Arden would have lost her mind years ago without Natalie and, more recently, Layla. Even Caroline, who'd only just met her, had said her talk with Arden left her feeling more unburdened than she had in a long time.

"I had a long chat with your mom." Breaking the

silence in the truck was far more jarring than she'd intended. Like a loud crash at midnight in a perfectly still house. Grimly determined, she plodded on. "It was very enlightening. I think if you heard what she had to say—"

"I'd what?" His head swiveled toward her, his tone lethal. "Stop caring that she betrayed her husband and her vows? Stop caring that I'm another man's bastard?"

"Well, no." She gulped, clinging to her resolve. "Arden, I don't want to talk about this."

"Maybe not, but you should, anyway. You can't just let it eat at you."

"Actually, I *can*. I don't answer to you."

Perhaps his scornful tone would have deterred another woman, but she'd had a lifetime of practice with stubborn males. She continued as if he hadn't spoken. "You know she messed up. What you don't know are the extenuating circumstances, what she was going through at the time."

"Yeah, you're an expert at justifying deception and questionable decisions. No surprise you're siding with her."

Anger boiled up in her. She'd been sincerely trying to help, and he'd thrown it back in her face, not even bothering to see the big picture. "Do you even know how freaking lucky you are to have a mother who loves you? Who's knocking herself out to win your forgiveness? Maybe I am siding with her—I'm *glad* she had the affair. Otherwise, you wouldn't be here. And I care about you, you jackass."

That stunned him into silence. The admission had come as a bit of a surprise to her, too.

After a moment, he snickered. "'I care about you, jackass'? You steal that from a greeting card?"

She tapped her head against the window. "I guess it's safe to conclude our child is gonna have something of a temper."

"A fair bet." A few minutes later, he added, "I shouldn't have taken your head off. The donor consultation yesterday left me in a foul mood. That's not your fault, and neither is what my mother did."

He didn't address the other part—when he'd accused her of deception and bad decisions. No matter how well they might get along at times, she was fooling herself if she allowed herself to believe for a second that what she'd done was behind them.

"I have to figure out what I'm going to tell my father if I check into the hospital for days on end. I *hate* having to lie to him. That's the part I can't forgive, you know. If she'd made an isolated mistake thirty-odd years ago, I'd like to think I'm a big enough person to let it go. But this isn't an obsolete aberration, it's ongoing. It's my life. We're lying to him every damn day. You think I'm a jerk because I haven't forgiven her yet? Well, I'm having trouble forgiving myself, too."

She squeezed his hand. "Garrett, you haven't done anything wrong."

"Really?" He flashed his teeth in a humorless smile. "Because it sure doesn't feel like I'm doing anything right. What would Dr. Mehta say about my arguing with you when we're supposed to be decreasing your blood pressure?"

"I promise not to rat you out," she said solemnly.

"You'll call me after the appointment Thursday,

won't you?" Garrett asked. "Put me out of my misery? Otherwise, I'll worry. Arden, I...care about you, too."

She wished he sounded happier about it, but, for now, she'd take what she could get.

ARDEN ALMOST THREW her arms around Dr. Mehta in an enthusiastic hug. Was that outside the bounds of an acceptable doctor-patient relationship? "So the baby and I are fine?"

Being a medical professional, he was hesitant to give a clear yes or no. They probably had to attend lawsuit avoidance seminars that trained them how to be so evasive. "Your blood pressure's still elevated above what I would like," he said, "but it's gone down since last week. We'll keep monitoring, but given the significant improvement, this probably isn't a serious condition. Get plenty of sleep and hydration, and watch your salt intake. Don't overexert yourself, and try to minimize stress."

They talked about her being scheduled to work a bar mitzvah Saturday afternoon, and he cleared her to proceed as scheduled, as long as she tried to take it easy for the first half of the day. Garrett's prediction that all she needed was a restorative weekend at the ranch may have been right on the money.

Once she reached her car in the parking lot, she scrolled through her contact list to find Garrett's name, grinning in anticipation of sharing the news.

"Hello?" He yelled the salutation over the considerable background noise of some kind of motor. "Arden, is that you?"

She pulled the phone away from her ear, raising her

voice so he could hear her. "Yep. Calling with important news. Guess whose blood pressure is down? This girl's!"

Even with the background motor noise, she clearly heard his sigh of relief. "We definitely have to celebrate when I come to town next week."

They'd decided that it made sense for Layla to remain her official labor coach since she lived locally and due dates were difficult to pinpoint. However, Garrett wanted to be part of the process and was planning to visit Cielo Peak to attend a couple of the birth classes. Arden couldn't believe how badly she was looking forward to seeing him. How was it possible to miss him so much after only a couple of days?

Even sleeping alone was more difficult after the two nights she'd spent cradled in his arms. He'd rubbed her back when she couldn't sleep, spoke to her in a low, drowsy murmur that seemed to even soothe the baby, taming some of Peanut's wilder, 3:00 a.m. somersaults. Would it be a mistake to tell Garrett he could stay with her instead of the Connors? Hugh and Darcy had generously offered their guest room on an as-needed basis for the duration of Arden's pregnancy.

"Thanks for taking the time to let me know," he told her.

"Hey, we're in this together." And not just the pregnancy. On Friday, she sent him several non-baby-related texts after a hilariously chaotic photo session with a family of seven. Then around eleven on Sunday night, Garrett texted her to find out if she was awake because he couldn't sleep. Upon discovering she was up, too, he called.

Arden lit a few candles in her otherwise dark bedroom and curled up in bed with some caramel-flavored hot chocolate and the phone.

"Is it too late to take you up on the offer to listen if I needed to talk about that kidney thing?" he asked.

Only a guy would call the generous act of giving part of yourself to save another human being's life *that kidney thing.* "The offer stands," she assured him.

"I've scheduled my check-in date for testing the week of Halloween. It's going to require time away from the ranch. Would I be a terrible person if I let Dad believe I was coming to see you?"

Understanding how much the dishonesty bothered him, she knew it had probably cost him something to ask. "I'm happy to be your alibi if you need one."

"Thanks. There's only so much lying I'm willing to do, though. I've made a decision, and I need a second opinion. If, after they finish the blood work and paperwork and mental evaluations, they conclude I'm not a good candidate, then I'll keep Mom's secret. Why hurt Dad with the truth? But if I go through with this organ donation, she's got to tell him. I could be looking at up to six weeks of not being able to do my usual activities around the ranch, and Dad's gonna need a reason. Kidney and cornea transplants are pretty commonplace, there's minimal risk to me."

For her own peace of mind, she'd needed to hear him reiterate that. If anything were to happen to *Garrett*...

"The possibilities of rejection and dangerous infection are on Will's end, but still, this is a major procedure. I can't lie to my father about it."

"I understand that. I imagine Caroline will, too. She knows more than anyone the kind of man she raised."

"It doesn't sound like extortion? You can have my kidney, but only if you bow to my wishes?"

"No. Just...try to be gentle with her. No one can go back in the past and undo their actions."

There was a long pause, and she squirmed inwardly, trying to picture his expression. Was he wistful? Bitter?

"If you *could* go back," he said, "would you have done things differently? Found me, told me about the baby?"

She bit the inside of her cheek. The easy answer was yes. Now that she knew what kind of man he was—and how lucky her child would be to have him for a father—of course she'd say yes. But she hadn't known then. "I can't change what happened, Garrett. I can only hope you forgive me."

He was silent, not the response she'd hoped for deep down, but an honest one.

Changing the subject, he asked if Peanut had settled for the night or was awake and active. "Would it be weird to hold the phone to your stomach and let me say good-night?"

"Yes. I'd feel like a fool."

He talked her into doing it, anyway, and she was smiling when they disconnected their call, mentally counting down the days until she'd see him again.

ARDEN'S FIRST BIRTH class was on a Wednesday evening, and she was touched that Garrett was making the trip even though he'd have to immediately turn around and go back. He and his father were driving to another ranch the next day to look at their herd and discuss trading some cattle. Garrett called her from the road to say he was running a few minutes behind and would meet her at the hospital.

True to his word, he pulled into the parking garage a few car lengths behind her. Her pulse stuttered in anticipation, and she smacked her palm to her forehead. She hadn't even seen him yet—was she really so far gone that she was reacting to the front bumper of his truck?

He came to her side while she was pulling out a duffel bag of supplies and a large pillow from home.

"How long's this session?" he teased, taking the duffel bag from her. "You look like you're planning to spend the night here."

"There are floor exercises. It said in the brochure to bring a blanket and pillow." They fell into step with each other and headed for the maternity wing. "Look, Garrett, I really appreciate your coming with me. I just hope you don't find these classes…silly. They're supposed to cover multiple types of birthing methods and new-age relaxation techniques. Some of it might get pretty touchy-feely."

He shot her a wicked grin. "Some of my favorite pastimes are of the touchy-feely variety."

She laughed, appreciating his easy, cheerful manner. He seemed far more himself now than when he'd brought her home last week. "Have you had a chance to talk to Caroline yet about your proposed compromise?" Maybe he was feeling lighter because they'd reached an agreement.

"Nope. Dad and I have actually been really busy, and since I won't have test results until November, there's not much to say to her on the subject." He reached forward to open the door for her.

"Things on the ranch must be going well. You seem pretty chipper," she observed.

His gaze met hers. "Maybe my good mood is just because I get to spend the evening with you."

And ten other couples, all of whom would be lying on the industrial-carpeted classroom floor, practicing pelvic positions and breathing. She grinned. If that was enough to put a spring in his step, then maybe she wasn't the only one falling hard.

The classroom was plastered with informational posters and smelled faintly of bleach. About half the pairs were already present and the instructor encouraged students to mingle and get to know one another. "No one can fully comprehend what new parents are going through quite like other new parents," she reminded them. "Make friends, compare notes."

Garrett and Arden were the only couple in this particular session who weren't husband and wife. Arden explained that Garrett was the baby's father and would be present for some of the weekly classes, but that her friend and labor coach Layla would attend the others. As they began the first set of exercises, Arden realized that it was going to be a little awkward with her friend here.

They did a take on "passive massage," where the men were supposed to lay their hands on their partners and visualize healing, supportive energy leaving their bodies and filling the mother's. Accompanied by the somewhat cliché recording of soft jazz interspersed with the sound of rolling waves and seagull cries, it could have been comical. But Garrett's touch made it an altogether different experience. She'd begun to crave his nearness the way some pregnant women ravenously craved peanut butter.

The exercise where she was supposed to mentally link with her cervix, however, was far less sensual. Finally, it was time to watch the evening's birth video. There would be one at every class, including footage of a water birth.

"Be warned, this may be pretty graphic," she whispered to Garrett as the instructor dimmed the lights.

"Not to compare you to livestock, but I have witnessed plenty of births. I know what to expect."

Yet ten minutes later, he was ashen. "It's different with cows," he mumbled when the class was dismissed. "I've never really thought about that happening to *you* before."

He seemed to be taking this hard—but this was nothing compared to what she imagined Layla's reaction would be to the explicit videos. *I'd better bring smelling salts with me next week.* She poked him in the shoulder. "Aren't I the one who's supposed to be a basket case?" she asked.

He looked chagrined. "Guess I wasn't really student of the week. Give me another chance?"

As many as it takes. "Of course. Besides, you did way better than that guy in the back who hyperventilated. Thanks again for coming with me. I owe you."

"Funny you should say that. I was actually planning to ask you a favor. Darcy's been requesting, rather insistently, that we consider a double date with them Sunday night."

Arden lost her footing for a second and grabbed his

arm to steady herself. She stopped on the sidewalk, turning to face him. "Now, when you say *date*..." There were so many butterflies in her stomach that there was hardly room left for the baby.

"I know we're coming at this a little backward, but what if we actually tried dating? It seems like the sensible thing to do for our kid, and we do like each other." His grin was lopsided as he tucked a strand of hair behind her ear. "That's how we found ourselves in this position, right?"

She'd admitted to herself that she was developing romantic feelings for him. Were those feelings mutual?

Maybe not yet. He'd said he *liked* her and that dating would be *sensible,* but that was a foundation, wasn't it? Could they try building a relationship and see where it led?

And if it doesn't work out? They would be linked together for their child's entire life. The stakes were considerably higher than when her brother had broken up with a waitress and made it temporarily uncomfortable to have lunch at his favorite barbecue house.

"C'mon, sweetheart," Garrett coaxed. "Is the idea of going out with me that repellent?"

Not repellent. Beguiling.

She nibbled at the inside of her lip. Was this wise? She tried to imagine what guidance she'd give to Layla, or Justin or, years from now, her own child. Strategic retreat, or embrace the possibilities?

"All right, you're on," she decided. "It's a date."

Chapter Eleven

"I think it's so romantic that you're dating now!" Layla winced when a string of hot glue adhered to her finger. "Of course, most women don't wait until they're seven months pregnant to enter a relationship with the baby's father, but you're a unique individual."

"Thanks, I think." Arden was watching her friend in morbid fascination. So far, Layla had burned herself twice and cut herself with a pair of extra-sharp craft fingers. "It might be premature to say we're *dating* since our first date isn't until tomorrow night."

"But you've talked every night this week."

True. She'd already been mentally filing funny observations from her morning with Layla to entertain him with during their conversation tonight. "Why again are you the one who has to make these—what do you call 'em?"

"*Calavera* masks. For the multicultural performance the drama students are doing. I can't tell you how thrilled I would be if the theater teacher got transferred to another district," she huffed. "Just because she had some minor parts in a couple of movies out in California, the principal and PTA indulge her every whim. Don't get me wrong, I'm all for the performance, but everyone else ends up rushing to do the work whenever she has one of these last-minute 'brainstorms.'"

Arden laughed at her friend's sequined air-quotes. Sparkly beads and bits of feathers clung to Layla's glue-scarred hands.

The two women sat at Layla's kitchen table, and a dozen skull masks covering the painted wood surface. Of the four that were already adorned, Arden had finished three of them.

"You really saved my butt, agreeing to do this," Layla said. "I asked two of my honors students, Melissa and Phillip, to help. They've been dating since freshman year. They're so inseparable, they have one of those unified monikers—you know, where people mash their names together? Philissa."

Arden carefully brushed glitter onto the swirling pattern she'd created with glue. "So where are they?"

"Officially, Melissa remembered an SAT prep class she had to attend this morning and he woke up with a fever. Unofficially? I overheard some arguing in the hall at school. She accused him of hitting on a JV cheerleader. Note to self, don't rely on hormonal teenage couples." Layla stopped abruptly. "Hey! If you and Garrett make it work, your name will be Garden."

"*This* is the thanks I get for spending my Saturday making arts-and-crafts skulls?" Arden asked dryly.

"What you have against gardens? Seems fitting to me." Layla chortled. "You guys are obviously fertile."

"You know what I just remembered? *I'm* supposed to be at that SAT prep class, too."

"If you stay," Layla declared, "you get to taste-test

the batch of Mexican wedding cookies I'm baking for after the performance."

"Done." Arden knew from experience that her friend's cookies were small, sugar-coated bites of heaven.

"Good, because there's something else we have to— damn it."

Laughing, Arden got out of her chair and reached for the hot glue gun. "Give that to me before we have to call 9-1-1."

"I have many impressive skills," Layla grumbled. "This just doesn't happen to be one of them. Okay, so about this other thing I wanted to discuss? Now that you two crazy kids have registered, I want to throw you a baby shower!"

"You do?" Arden was touched.

"Duh. That's what friends do for each other. That and make Day of the Dead masks, even though Day of the Dead isn't technically until November first. It sounds like Garrett enjoys being involved in planning for the baby, so I thought he'd like to come. But I don't think it should be specifically a couples' shower, since that would count me out. And both your brothers."

"You want my brothers to attend?" Arden asked skeptically. Colin would be visibly uncomfortable, a pall on the festivities, whereas Justin would be like a kid in a candy store, unabashedly flirting with any female guests. Too bad she couldn't invite his ex-girlfriend Elisabeth. She and Arden had been close until the breakup.

"Your brothers are your family. I know how critical family is to you."

That was indisputable. "Okay, so they go on the invite list. Who else are we thinking? Vivian Pike, for sure." Viv managed the personalized print store next door to Arden's studio. She specialized in customized stationery and cute business cards. "And Hugh and Darcy Connor." Not only had they been the reason Arden and Garrett met in the first place, but it would also be nice for Garrett to have some friends there.

Thinking of Garrett made her question the timing. In late October, he would be in the hospital. If he decided to through with the donation, she had no idea what the potential timetable for the transplant was. If they were going to have this shower, sooner might be better than later.

"Layla, I know it doesn't give people much notice, but if we keep it on the casual side, is this the type of thing that could be put together in a couple of weeks?"

"Are you kidding?" Her friend swept a hand majestically over the table. "Last-minute rush jobs are my specialty. As long as I don't have to hot-glue anything for your party, we're golden."

GARRETT COULDN'T REMEMBER the last time he'd been nervous picking a woman up for a date. After all the time he'd spent with Arden, it was insane to feel nervous now. *No more insane than taking the mother of your child on a first date.* Maybe "sane" wasn't really their thing.

He parked his truck in her driveway, thinking that his dad was partly to blame for his anxious tension. Before Garrett had left the Double F, his father had resumed hounding him about marrying Arden, urging Garrett to hurry.

"I don't get why you're dragging your feet," Brandon had scolded. "She's a great gal, and you know it. Do you want your kid to be illegitimate?"

Why not? Garrett had thought sourly. *I was.*

Garrett had always assumed he'd get married someday. He just wanted to find the right person, the way his parents had. It was sobering to think that, as many years as they'd been together, as much as they loved each other, Caroline had been unfaithful. How could a relationship between two people with such a solid foundation go so wrong? He was glad he and Arden were going to give a relationship a try, but that didn't mean he was naive. He knew there were bound to be mistakes and regrets lying in wait for them.

Which was hardly the right attitude to begin their date.

He pasted a polite smile on his face that became a real one as soon as she opened the door. God, she was lovelier every time he saw her. He suddenly wanted to kick himself for not bringing flowers.

Her gaze swept from his head to his feet, and she beamed at him. "Wow. You clean up well. Not that you aren't equally attractive in a coat and cowboy hat, but... wow. Am I underdressed?"

"No. You're perfect. And my clothes aren't *that* dressy." Okay, he'd swapped his usual jeans for black slacks and got a haircut yesterday, but it wasn't like he'd shown up in a tie.

She wore an ankle-length maternity dress in deep green. The color made her eyes damn near mesmerizing.

"You look gorgeous," he told her as he stepped inside. The words weren't very suave or creative, but there was enough ragged appreciation in his voice that she couldn't doubt his sincerity.

"Well, I'm glad we were both in the same ballpark. When I told you to surprise me with our destination, I didn't realize I was making my wardrobe choice so difficult."

"You could have called to ask for hints, like whether we were going to be outside or whether the venue was formal."

"That felt like cheating somehow." She tilted her head. "So where *are* we going?"

"You'll see. Hugh and Darcy are meeting us there." Part of him worried that adding another couple made the evening less romantic, as if he wasn't trying hard enough, but he wanted Arden to get to know the Connors better. He liked the idea that they could look in on her if Garrett were unable to come to town for long stretches.

"Don't let me forget to tell them about our shower! Official invitations will go out later."

He frowned. "Shower?"

"Ah, I jumped ahead—sorry. Guess I temporarily forgot to invite you to the baby shower. It's on my list of things to talk about tonight."

He laughed. "You have a list?"

"Um…" She stared at the floor. "I'd like to say that was a figure of speech, but if someone were to check the memo section on my phone, they might find actual bullet points. You don't understand what pregnancy brain is like! I had to fill out a form the other day, and I blanked on my own address. So, yeah, I may have jotted down a few reminders of things that happened this week I thought you'd get a kick out of. It made me feel calmer, like I had some backup ammo in case we hit any awkward silences. Does this make me sound like a lunatic who doesn't know how to be spontaneous?"

"It makes you sound well-prepared and thoughtful." Qualities that were going to make her a great mom. Scratch that—qualities that made her a great person. They'd been so fixated on the pregnancy lately, their excitement for the baby, that he had to remind himself to stop and just enjoy *her*. Starting with tonight.

He stepped behind her to help her into her coat and resisted the urge to pull her body back against his. Her soft curves were tempting, but this was their first date and he wanted to be on time for meeting the Connors. "Ready to have a wonderful time?"

ARDEN WAS SO busy absorbing her surroundings that she didn't hear the hostess the first time she offered to take their coats. "Oh! Yes, please." She shrugged out of the red wool jacket.

She and Garrett had arrived first. They were spending their evening at a dinner theater called the Twirling Mustache Tavern. Arden had been here once, years ago, to see a musical with Natalie. But the Tavern was actually known for its uproariously over-the-top melodramas. Audience participation was strongly encouraged.

Theatergoers were expected to cheer loudly for the hero, yell catchphrases along with the actors and greet any romantic moments with a synchronized "aww." But according to the playbill she'd been handed, the villains got the lion's share of the attention. Patrons could not only boo and hiss when a mustache-twirling bad guy tied a heroine to the train tracks or evicted a little old lady from her farm, but each table was also given a huge bucket of popcorn they were supposed to throw at the stage during evil deeds. House rules asked that customers *only* throw the popcorn, and not the actual bucket. It all sounded like a blast and, despite her emergency list of topics in case of awkward silence, she doubted silence of any kind would be a problem.

They explained to the hostess that friends would be joining them shortly and were escorted to a table for four very close to the stage.

"I don't know how well you got to know them when they hired you for the wedding, but I think you'll really like Hugh and Darcy. Although, word of warning?" Garrett said. "Darcy is a dedicated—one might even say, zealous—bird-watcher. If the subject happens to come up, we may be hearing about it for a while. Like, until November."

Arden chuckled. "So no mentioning birds, even in passing."

"To be extra safe, we probably shouldn't order the duck or chicken. But other than that one tiny quirk, the Connors are great."

"It would be pretty hypocritical of us to judge anyone for being quirky." She gave him a rueful smile. "We're not exactly the poster children for normal. How many men take a woman home to meet his parents before he's even been on a date with her?"

He brandished a piece of popcorn at her. "Are you saying I'm abnormal?"

"Psst!" Hugh Connor stopped at their table, his voice

a faux whisper. "I know you said you were out of practice at this, buddy, but generally speaking, it's not chivalrous to throw things at your date."

Behind him, Darcy was nodding in agreement. "I suppose you could make a possible exception for rose petals, but even then she might find it odd." She craned her head around her husband and waggled her fingers in hello. "A pleasure to see you again, Arden."

It turned out that Darcy and Hugh were regulars at the Tavern, and they recommended some of their favorite entrees. The food was delicious, but Garrett's smiles throughout the dinner were far more tantalizing than anything on the menu. Arden had enjoyed her time at the Double F with Garrett and his family, but there was no denying that being around his parents had caused him stress. Here in the presence of an old friend, no secrets to be kept or emotional baggage to overcome, Garrett was relaxed and witty.

What am I going to do? The more she saw of Garrett, the more she discovered to love about him. Her heart went out to the taciturn cowboy who was struggling with his sense of loyalty to each parent. But her heart absolutely melted for the charming date who knew all the right things to say and never failed to signal the waitress if Arden's glass of water was even close to getting empty. He was gallant and funny and caring. She couldn't think of any qualities she might want in a man that Garrett Frost didn't have in abundance.

Except maybe forgiveness? Against her will, she recalled how icy he'd been when Arden had tried to broker peace between him and his mother. While he seemed to be making gradual progress, it was slow. How long would it take his anger to fully dissipate? And what about Arden herself? He'd asked the other night if she'd do things differently, and he hadn't seemed pleased with her answer.

But those were needless worries. For now, they were having a fantastic evening together, and there was no reason to dwell on negative issues he might be well on his way to resolving.

During a particularly "dastardly" scene in the play, Garrett heckled the villain louder than anyone else in the audience, mercilessly pelting him with pieces of popcorn since he was at such close range. Without ever breaking in dialogue, the actor stepped down from the stage and upended the bucket of popcorn on Garrett's head. Arden and Darcy both burst into laughter, and Hugh choked on his beer.

Garrett laughed as hard as any of them, and the amusement in his silvery eyes gave her hope. He didn't look like a man consumed with anger.

Once the play ended, Darcy asked if they wanted to join her and Hugh at a coffeehouse that was open late and featured independent musicians. Arden thanked her for the invitation but admitted she was tired, then told the Connors she looked forward to seeing them at the baby shower.

The ride home nearly lulled her to sleep, but when Garrett walked her to her door, she was instantly, eagerly, awake. Her heart thundered. Surely he'd kiss her good-night? They'd kissed each other even when they *weren't* dating.

"Did you, um, want to come in for a drink?" she asked breathlessly.

He shook his head. "No drink necessary, but the gentlemanly thing would be to see you safely inside." The wolfish grin he gave her beneath the front porch light made her think *gentlemanly* wasn't what he had in mind.

Once they made it to the foyer, he tugged her into his arms, his lips greedily claiming hers as if he'd been waiting to do this all night. She certainly had. Exquisite sensation blossomed inside her, hot and liquid. He speared his tongue into her mouth, making her light-headed with pleasure. When he pulled back, she almost whimpered in protest.

"I promised myself I would kiss you good-night and leave," he confided.

"Already?"

"If we keep this up, sweetheart…" With a groan of surrender, he took her mouth again. Her jacket hit the floor, and his hand slid down from the curve of her shoulder to cup her breast. She sucked his lower lip in fervent approval.

And the baby picked that moment to kick—although it felt more like a cannon blast than a foot motion.

Arden could feel her cheeks reddening as she stepped back. *Way to kill the mood, Junior.*

Garrett's eyes glowed with humor. "Is that kind of like the kid walking into the room and catching his parents making out?"

"Pretty talented, considering ours can't even walk." She managed to laugh in spite of her frustrated libido.

He palmed her cheek. "I should go."

"You don't *have* to. We spent the night together at the ranch," she reminded him.

"Not after kissing like that, we didn't. I stay, you might not get much sleep."

Sounds good to me. She knew her need for him was clear on her face—not to mention pulsing through other parts of her body.

He swore under his breath. "I'm not made of steel. We agreed to date, and I want to do this right. You pointed out the steps we've skipped, how we've done everything out of order up until now, and I think it's too important to be rushed. I want to send you roses tomorrow to thank you for a great time, start planning where I can take you next, call you during the week to let you know I'm thinking about you. I want to court you. You deserve that."

She let out a dreamy sigh. "That is the most romantic rejection I have ever heard in my life."

TRUE TO HIS word, Garrett did call her all during the next week—often right around bedtime. It quickly became her favorite part of the day. Hearing from him always gave her that little rush of exhilaration, but it was different at night, more intimate, less hurried. She curled up in the dark, closed her eyes and lost herself in his voice, pretending he was there with her.

He wasn't able to come to Cielo Peak the following weekend because he was managing the ranch while his parents were in Denver. Caroline was shopping in the city while Brandon attended a conference on winter grazing. Who knew there were such things? Arden had always pictured ranchers giving each other sage advice over fence lines, not holed up in the conference room of a Denver hotel, reviewing PowerPoint presentations about sod, rye and clover.

"But next weekend, when I come to town for the shower, I'll make it up to you by staying several nights," Garrett promised.

The Friday night before the shower, he called to tell her he couldn't wait to see her the next day. "I miss you."

"Want to prove it? When you stay in town this weekend, stay with me," she pleaded. "I don't want to be alone after the shower. I'll be all weepy over cute little outfits, and there will be nursery equipment I'll be impatient to assemble. I know you don't want me attempting to build furniture on my own."

He chuckled. "That's blackmail."

"Mmm, actually I think it's coercion," she said unrepentantly. Then, more seriously, she asked, "Will you at least think about it? Spending the night here could be your shower present to me."

"What makes you think I don't already have a present?"

"Really?" She spent a few minutes trying to wheedle clues out of him while he taunted her in classic juvenile I-know-something-you-don't-know fashion.

"So tell me again who's on the guest list for this shower?" he asked. "It feels surreal that I'll be celebrating the arrival of our baby with some people I've never even met."

"But you'll know the Connors and Layla, plus my brothers will be there." She got momentarily sidetracked. "I *wanted* to invite Elisabeth Donnelly. She's Justin's ex-girlfriend. They were great together, but she was the godmother for her college roommate's daughter.

When her former roommate passed away, Elisabeth got custody of the little girl. The situation was too intense for my brother. I adore Justin, but he needs to grow up. If he had any sense at all, he'd get her back. I asked him if I could invite Elisabeth but he refused. I should have just asked her to come and not told him."

"You would've blindsided him? In the middle of our shower?"

"For his own good. You don't understand. He makes jokes all the time, but his happiness is superficial. Deep down, in his own way, I think he's nearly as miserable as Colin. He could benefit from someone scheming on his behalf."

"But not telling him she was coming would be the same as lying to him." Garrett's tone had taken on an edge. "You can't deceive someone just because you think you know what's best!"

She inhaled sharply, stung by his anger.

"If we're going to be in a relationship, Arden, I have to know you aren't going to rationalize away my right to the truth whenever it suits you."

"And *I* have to know that you can get past this!" She could only apologize so many times. "You had every right to be upset that I kept the pregnancy a secret, but I can't change that. And we weren't even discussing us, we were talking about my brother. I know my family a lot better than you do."

"Oh, really? Because you keep trying to pin Colin down and make him stay put. You don't seem as interested in what he needs as you do in keeping him close because it's what you need."

The implication that she was selfish sent her reeling. She adored her brothers and wanted the very best for them. Especially Colin! How many eighteen-year-old boys put their lives on hold to raise an annoying kid sister?

"You don't understand what it's like to have brothers or sisters," she shot back. "And you sure as hell don't seem to understand *me*."

With a muttered "Guess not," he told her he'd see her at the shower and ended the call.

"OH, HOW I WISH the punch was spiked," Arden lamented.

"If it was," Layla reminded her, "you couldn't have any."

"Maybe we could use it to sedate Garrett. Assuming he's even coming."

Layla paused in the middle of removing a plastic baby bottle from its packaging. "He'll be here. You guys had a fight—it happens. You're pregnant, with a hormonal probability of turning cranky, and it was late at night. He could've been tired and overreacted. Honestly, it was one argument. That's nothing compared to the kinds of things the two of you have endured. Together and separately."

"Lord, I hope you're right." Arden had lain awake for hours last night, rotating between crying jags, righteous fury and the almost visceral need to call him back.

"Of course I'm right! Now help me open the rest of these bottles."

"Why are there so many?" Arden asked. "Don't tell me these are what the guests will be drinking out of."

"Ha! No, these are for baby bottle bowling. Because

yours truly is a genius, I planned all games where the equipment needed is actually extra baby supplies for you guys. Once I've got these all opened, where can I set up my lanes?"

They'd discussed having the shower at Layla's house, since she was the hostess and didn't want to create any extra work or cleaning for the mommy-to-be. But they'd decided it was silly to have everyone bring presents to her house when Arden and Garrett would simply have to load them back up for transport home. So Layla had come over bright and early to help Arden tidy up—and to listen to her vent about last night's catastrophic phone call.

"It started off so well," Arden said in disbelief. "He was as happy to be talking with me as I was with him. How did we make such a mess of it?"

"Sometimes phone conversations are more difficult than face-to-face. Long distance is hard, but you guys will get the hang of it."

How? After the baby was born, she'd be exhausted from middle-of-the-night feedings and barely be able to stay awake for their nocturnal chats—and that was assuming that a crying infant didn't make it impossible to hear. She'd adored her nephew, Danny, but when he'd been an infant, some of his ear-splitting crying spells had gone on for thirty minutes straight. Even if she and Garrett eventually mastered long-distance dating... to what end? What was their ultimate goal here? That she'd live in Cielo Peak, he'd work the ranch all week and they'd only be a family on weekends? Her memories of her own parents were faded with time, but she remembered two people very much in love.

Family was the most important thing in the world. Didn't her child deserve more than parents who were in a part-time relationship?

"Hey!" Layla snapped her fingers. "I know that look. Guests will be here within the hour. This is not a good time to fall apart. Besides, you know that if Justin and Colin get here and find you red-eyed over Garrett, they'll use it as an excuse to pick a fight with him."

"Good point." Telling herself that Layla had gone to a lot of trouble to make today special, Arden got busy slicing up cucumbers for the cucumber-and-cream-cheese appetizers. The *whack whack whack* of the knife against the cutting board was cathartic, and by the time the doorbell rang, she no longer wanted to cry. Much.

She found Garrett at her front door, holding an armful of gold bags—her favorite chocolate and caramel medallions.

"I bought out three different stores," he told her. "Can you forgive me? I know you love your brothers, and you were only speaking hypothetically."

"Only if you'll forgive me, too. I should've been more tolerant of your point of view." She threw her arms around him, although he was holding too much candy to return the hug. "I'm so glad you're here. I was afraid you'd change your mind."

"And miss today? This is our first real family event. Wild horses couldn't have kept me away. Now, would you like to relieve me of some of this chocolate? Because I still have to unload all the real gifts from the truck."

As he brought in prettily wrapped pastel packages and gift bags, Layla mouthed a gloating *told you so* in

Arden's direction. Arden merely laughed. She'd never been so elated to be wrong.

Shortly thereafter, Justin arrived, asking if there was anything he could do to help. He made jokes with Layla and Arden and was even passably friendly to Garrett. But when he and Arden were alone in the kitchen, his good-humored mask fell away, revealing sorrow.

"Don't shoot the messenger," he said. "But I bring tidings from our brother."

"He isn't coming?" She was as unsurprised as she was disappointed.

"I tried for over an hour to talk him into it, telling him it's what our parents would have wanted—for him to be here since they can't—but nothing worked."

"Thanks for making the effort. Maybe…maybe it is better for him not to be here." She didn't want to flaunt her burgeoning new happiness in front of Colin, and the baby shower she had once thrown for him and Natalie would probably have been etched in his mind all day. Replaying Garrett's words from the night before, she tried to focus on what her brother needed for his mental well-being. Maybe some men were like wounded animals, needing to skulk off on their own before they could heal. She resolved to stop smothering him with her worry.

The Connors' arrival was a welcome distraction. As it turned out, Darcy was nearly as besotted with babies as she was with birds. She cooed over the decorations, the planned games, the adorable gift tags on the presents that were piling up in front of the fireplace. And she kept reminding Arden and Garrett that after the baby was born, they had a ready and waiting babysitter.

"And that is officially the last time I say the *B*-word," Darcy vowed as she handed a diaper pin over to Layla. One of the ongoing shower games was that everyone fastened a diaper pin to their clothes, and if they were heard saying the word *baby,* another guest could claim the pin. Whoever had collected the most by the end of the party won a mystery door prize.

The final guests showed up, including Vivian Pike and Nurse Sonja from the hospital. As with all parties since the beginning of time, everyone ended up gathered around the snack table.

Justin grinned at the nurse he'd briefly dated. "Good to know that if this shindig gets too wild, we have a medical professional on the premises in case of emergency."

When Sonja asked Arden if she was sticking to her guns about not learning the gender ahead of time, Darcy followed up by saying, "Are you making lists of potential girls' names *and* potential boys' names?"

"I can help with that," Justin volunteered. "The name Justin, for example, is majestic and traditional. Teachers won't misspell it, kids won't pick on it. Also good are Justine and Justina for girls."

Garrett made a show of leaning toward Arden and whispering much too loudly, "Remind me why we invited him."

"Because we feel sorry for him." She smirked. "He's alienated all the women in a hundred-mile radius and thus has no social life."

"That is patently untrue," Justin argued. He turned to Vivian, who fell into the rare category of both being single and having never dated him. "For instance, have I alienated you yet? Justin Cade, nice to meet you."

They followed bottle bowling with an entertainingly ridiculous scavenger hunt and a baby-changing relay race where team members had to strip one outfit off of a baby doll and get a completely different one all snapped into place as quickly as possible.

"And Arden gets to keep all these clothes," Layla added. "I went with gender-neutral colors like yellow, which is just as easily masculine as feminine."

"The hell it is," Garrett whispered for Arden's ears only. He obviously didn't think buttercup-yellow would be suitable attire for a son.

From across the room, Justin gave them a thumbs-up, as if he knew what Garrett had said and agreed whole-heartedly. It was the first sign of real bonding Arden had witnessed between the men, and it was heartening to think they might not kill each other, after all.

Layla sliced up the decadent cake she'd ordered from Arden's favorite local bakery, and the guests found spots in the cramped living room to enjoy dessert while watching her open gifts.

The Connors had purchased an adorable play mat la-beled a "baby gym," and Arden laughed. "Did Garrett tell you our child is already an Olympian in training?" Garrett's parents went overboard with their gifts, which included both the stroller and the playpen from the registry. Arden rolled her eyes at Justin's present, infant shirts with slogans like Cuteness Runs in the Family. You Should Meet My Uncle.

"You are *not* using my kid to scam women," she said. He laughed, then handed her a card with Colin's handwriting on it. "He asked me to deliver this." He lowered his voice. "I know he hates himself for not being here. He just couldn't."

Oh, what she wouldn't give to wave a magic wand and erase Colin's pain. If Colin needed to go somewhere else in order to eventually find his way back to them, she would support that. As she read the card he'd signed, sentimental tears welled in her eyes, then she gasped when she saw the amount of the gift card he'd placed in the envelope.

Garrett was equally startled. "Whoa. Is this to help pay for newborn provisions, or is he single-handedly trying to put the kid through college?"

After everyone else's presents had been unwrapped, Garrett handed her a gift bag that he said was from him. "Nothing off the registry," he said. "Just a little something all kids should have."

She reached inside and pulled out a baby-size supersoft, red cowboy hat that inexplicably made her cry. It would be adorable on either a little boy or girl. There was also a chocolate-brown floppy plush cow.

"These are the sweetest things I've ever seen." She sniffled. She hugged the plush stuffed animal to her chest.

"Took me a while to find one that wasn't black-and-white. They shouldn't all be Holsteins!" Garrett complained. The man was serious about his cows.

She thanked him with a hug, but had other ideas about how she wanted to thank him once they were alone. It was Darcy Connor who seemed to guess Arden's feelings and subtly began directing guests to leave. Justin left with Vivian, and Arden didn't know whether to be amused or irritated. Finally, only Layla was left.

As the two of them straightened the kitchen, Arden told her, "You outdid yourself with the food. No one who was here will need to cook dinner tonight."

In between his trips carrying all the gifts to the eventual nursery, Garrett thanked Layla with a hug and a kiss on the cheek, flustering her.

"Sorry," Layla whispered to Arden. "I know he's yours, but damn, he's hot."

Finally, *finally,* it was just Arden and Garrett. Alone at last after she hadn't seen him for two weeks. Taking his hand, she led him to the couch but didn't sit with him.

"You never actually gave me a straight answer when I asked you on the phone. Are you staying tonight?" she asked shyly.

He nodded, his gray eyes intense. "The entire drive to Cielo Peak, I worried that I'd lost my chance to build something with you. I need to hold you, feel you with me."

Leaning forward, she kissed him tenderly. "Then we're definitely on the same page. Wait here?" she murmured near his ear.

Battling the impulse to race to her closet in an undignified sprint, she sauntered out of the room, giving him a sassy wink over her shoulder.

As often as she thought about him during the days and nights when he wasn't in town, she'd had ample time to play this out in her mind. While she didn't think of herself as specifically vain, any woman seducing a man wanted to look her best. No way in hell was she letting him peel industrial-strength maternity undergarments off of her. At least, not for their first time.

And, in a way, this would be their first time.

What seemed like a lifetime ago, she'd had sex with a good-looking and very kind cowboy who'd changed her life forever. But now, she was about to make love to Garrett, the man she'd come to know over the past month, the man who worked hard and knew how to make her laugh, the man who cherished family as much as she did, the man who acted as if he'd do battle to defend her honor but looked completely at home holding a snuggly stuffed cow.

She'd purchased a very simple nightgown. The silky material was midnight-blue and fell from spaghetti straps to hit right above her knees. It wasn't ornate or lacy or sheer, but it made her feel sexier than she had in months.

Wearing nothing but the nightgown, she returned to the living room. Her senses were so heightened that the mere brush of satiny fabric against bare skin was arousing.

Garrett sat bolt upright, shock and pure masculine hunger playing across his face. "This may have been a strategic mistake on your part," he cautioned. "If this is what I get after we argue…well, I may be picking a lot of fights."

She smiled but didn't say anything as she continued her unhurried approach.

He leaned toward her, catching her waist in his hands and tipping her almost off balance as he pulled her forward. She thudded against him, soft and curved in all the places he was hard, and his heat went straight through the thin material.

He threaded one hand through her hair, angling her head to deepen their kiss until it felt as if they were fused together. Sensation built in the very core of her. Dazed, she realized that she'd begun rocking against his lap. He bit her earlobe, not hard enough to hurt, but just enough to penetrate the sweet hazy fog of desire enveloping her.

"Are you sure about this, sweetheart?" He took her chin in his hand, meeting her eyes and seeking assurance.

"Completely. All the stuff we unwrapped earlier is wonderful, but this is the only gift I really wanted today."

Needing no further urging, he reached down to tug off his belt while she fumbled with the buttons on his shirt. When he was stripped down to dark boxer-briefs, he repositioned her on his lap, kissing her like a man in a frenzy, leaving her mouth only to skim kisses across her sensitive collarbone. Meanwhile, his fingers traced maddening circles over her breast, not yet touching the sensitive peak. Without warning, he replaced his hand with his mouth, suckling her through the silky nightgown.

She cried out, her inner muscles clenching, tension already spiraling through her, pooling low where she was wet and wanting. Under his skillful attention, it wouldn't take long for her to detonate in his arms. *"Garrett."* She clutched the back of the sofa with one hand, crushing the upholstery in her fingers as she ground against him. He was hard as stone beneath her.

"Right there with you, sweetheart." As he shifted the hem of her nightgown to position himself, the straps slid down her shoulders. He tugged them farther, exposing her breasts to the cool air as he flexed his hips upward to enter her. He went slowly at first, not penetrating completely, savoring the moment and giving her time to adjust. But then he gripped her hips and thrust, wrenching another ecstatic scream from her. Her nerve endings were on fire with need. Using the back of the couch for leverage, she moved with abandon until the mounting tension began to ripple and spasm and finally exploded outward with such force it nearly blinded her for a second.

With a shout, he plunged into her one last time, then cuddled her against his chest.

Eventually, she realized she was practically panting and cursed herself for not having the forethought to place a glass of water nearby. "That…" She couldn't quite catch her breath enough to finish her sentence. But that was okay. There were no words adequate enough to capture what they'd just shared.

Chapter Twelve

Pale October sunshine stole through the window, and Arden experienced a childish urge to hide underneath her sheets. She resented that it was morning already and expressed her opinion with a rude noise along the lines of a raspberry.

Next to her, Garrett propped himself on one elbow. "You don't have to get up yet, you know. I realize some insensitive SOB kept you up half the night."

More than half, but that wasn't why she was feeling peevish. "I'm not tired. I just don't want... You're like a living, breathing sci-fi anomaly."

His eyebrows drew together. "Is that some sort of compliment on my performance? If so, I'll take it. But I don't get it."

"I think you disrupt the flow of time somehow. Whenever you're around, time flies so quickly it's unnatural. Then when you're gone...it feels like whole civilizations rise and crumble in the days when I don't see you."

He sifted his fingers through her hair. "I miss you, too."

When he climbed out of bed to take a shower, he invited her to join him, but she was feeling too blue to thoroughly appreciate the experience. He paused in the bathroom doorway. "You *are* going to be here when I get out, right? No running off and leaving me a note?"

That succeeded in drawing a smile. "One of the benefits of having sex with a woman in her own home is that she's unlikely to flee afterward. Of course, one of the drawbacks is that there's no room service."

"Don't be so sure," he told her. "I saw eggs in your fridge last night. You stay put, and think about what you want in your omelet. I owe you a breakfast in bed."

Thirty minutes later, he made good on his promise. He sat against her headboard, shirtless and barefoot, while she snuggled next to him in her favorite robe. She only had one breakfast tray, so both of their plates were balanced on it, giving them an excuse for extra closeness.

She moaned her appreciation at the fluffy, perfectly seasoned eggs. "This is terrific. How am I going to let you leave?"

"Maybe you don't have to. I did a lot of thinking while I was cooking. Dad always said I was stubborn, but I guess his lectures are finally sinking in."

She wasn't exactly following his train of thought, but as soon as he'd said maybe he didn't have to go, her heart had thumped happily. "You don't need to return back to the ranch soon?"

"No, I do. It's my job, and my life. I explained it wrong. When I leave, what if you came with me? My dad's been telling me since the day he met you that if I had the brains God gave a turnip, I'd take you off the market once and for all."

She gave him an incredulous look. "Off the market?"

"Marry you. And he's right."

"You can't be serious." Her brain whirled. What had happened to "let's not rush this" and "you deserve to be courted"? Okay, yes, they'd taken a big step forward last night, but she hadn't realized it was tantamount to getting engaged.

"Of course I am. I wouldn't joke about this." He swung his feet over the side of the bed, and she knew he'd be pacing within minutes. "Our baby received so many presents yesterday. Wouldn't the best gift be a stable home, a mother and father under one roof? We both know how important family is. Don't you want to provide that for the little one?"

She resented that line of reasoning. It sounded too much like he was trying to guilt her into the biggest decision of her life.

"It's the smart thing to do," he pronounced, irritating her even more.

"So if I don't say yes, I'm dumb *and* a bad mother?"

"What? How the hell did you make that leap?" He narrowed his eyes. "Wait, why wouldn't you say yes? We've both wondered how we're going to make this work long distance. You're alone here. At the Double F there's someone who can share the middle-of-the-night changings, built-in babysitting so you can keep working. Or you could stop working. I'll take care of you."

Now she shot out of the bed, too. It was a reminder of everything intimate they'd shared during the night— back *before* she'd wanted to throttle him—and she didn't want to acknowledge those memories right now. "I'm not alone here! I have Justin and Layla and my studio. And, yes, I plan to keep working. I love being a photographer, and I spent a lot of time building a professional reputation and cultivating word-of-mouth marketing. You would expect me to drop all of that without a second thought?"

Apparently, he would. He *had*.

He ran a hand through his hair, making it stand on end. It looked as stressed out as she was feeling. "Is this really so out of the blue, so unthinkable? In less than two months, you're having my baby. In a perfect world, we'd have more time to plan and discuss, but we didn't go about any of this perfectly."

Irrational tears burned her eyes. Last night had seemed pretty damned perfect. For that matter, she'd accumulated a number of "perfect moment" memories in Garrett's presence, even when it had been something as small as laughing until her face hurt over the world's ugliest souvenir pen. But to hear him tell it, he'd merely been making the best of a bad situation.

Suddenly devoid of energy, she sank back down to the mattress. "You said your father's been goading you to get married since the day he met me? We weren't even dating then."

"True, but he knew we were about to be parents. If we get married before Thanksgiving, our child will—"

"*Before* Thanksgiving?" Was he delusional? They'd never even discussed this before now, and he wanted to throw together a wedding in five or six weeks? Tears burned her eyes. He'd gone from telling his family there was "nothing romantic" between them to insisting she become his wife. Obviously marriage meant very different things to each of them. "Garrett, why do you want to marry me?"

"I told you. The baby des—"

"My answer is no."

GARRETT HAD LEFT Cielo Peak in a raging bad mood that did not improve on his drive to the ranch. Arden had been unreasonable. She'd admitted she was miserable without him, but she refused to take the logical step so that they could be together. Even though it would make them both happy. Even though it was best for the baby.

Despite knowing his parents would want to hear about the shower and ask how she'd liked their gifts, he drove straight past their house. He needed to be alone. But fate had something different in mind. He'd barely removed his boots when his doorbell rang. He held his breath, debating how to proceed. He couldn't really ignore his own parents the way one might a door-to-door salesman.

"Son?" Brandon called. "We need to talk to you. It's important."

It had better not be about Arden. He'd had enough of his father's unsolicited advice on that front. *I tried, Dad.* She'd trampled his proposal with all the violence of a stampeding herd.

Years of ingrained obedience won out, and he opened the door for his father. Garrett did a double take, noting that his mom had been crying and that even his father's eyes were puffy. He experienced a moment of emotional vertigo— Oh, God. Had Will Harlow lost his battle with renal failure? "C-come in." Garrett cast his hand out to the side blindly, looking for something that would steady him.

They filed into the living room, no one speaking,

until finally, Caroline said, in a voice so small it was almost inaudible, "Your father suggested that we invite Will for Thanksgiving next month. He has no family, and he's been so ill. It would be the charitable thing to do. And I just…couldn't. I couldn't go on not telling him anymore."

This wasn't about a downturn in the man's health? This was about Thanksgiving? Garrett's gaze dropped, zeroing in on his parents' joined hands. They were here as a unified front? Brandon hadn't driven into the mountains to process news of his wife's duplicity?

"You're not mad?" Garrett asked without thinking. "You don't care?"

"Of course I care, son. Especially for you. Your momma tells me you've been going through hell this last month, and I've never been prouder of you. You want to help a man who's critically ill, despite your anger. You tried to protect your momma by keeping her secret, but through it all, you've felt a strong pull of loyalty to me? We raised you good. And you had reason to be hurt. But only the two people *in* a relationship can truly understand what's happening between them."

Sometimes even fewer than two. Garrett, for one, had no idea why Arden had thrown away what could have been an amazing future.

"You don't know what that time was like for Caro, what I was like. I have a son, and Will may be dying. In light of those facts, holding a grudge seems pretty pointless. We just wanted you to know you don't have to hide it anymore. And we both fully support whatever you decide about the kidney donation. Suffice to say, Will Harlow won't be joining us for Thanksgiving.

Not that I suppose it makes much difference to you. We figure you'll be in Cielo Peak."

With Arden, they meant. It was going to be difficult to feel thankful after her rejection.

Despite his relief over Brandon finally knowing the truth and his admiration that his parents had managed to weather such a significant betrayal, Garrett felt hollow. How could he be this bereft? When he'd first learned about Pea—about the baby, he'd assumed he and Arden would parent separately and platonically. It was only very recently that he'd begun to believe they could have more. They'd been on *one* date. How could he mourn the loss of something he'd never truly had?

His gaze went involuntarily to his parents' still-linked hands. Just because he'd never had something didn't mean he couldn't recognize the value of it.

THREE TEENAGERS POSED against a pumpkin-patch backdrop in Halloween costumes ranging from zombie cheerleader to a two-headed mummy. But the scariest thing in the studio was Arden's unshakable gloom. What was the point in a soon-to-be mom taking a principled stand on her right to keep working if she chased off all her clients with her morose attitude?

"Great shots, girls." She put the camera away, trying not to think about when she and Natalie had been that age, the silly moments like these—funny BFF photos, staging "chance" run-ins with boys they liked, never having any idea the twists and turns their lives would take.

After the giggling teens had chipped in their money and selected the photo they wanted for their joint package, Arden was alone—free to put her head on her desk and cry her guts out. Except she couldn't. The woman who'd cried at greeting cards, soup commercials, random puppies she passed in the park and internet banner ads was completely empty. She'd been dry-eyed since Garrett stomped out of her house last week, unable to wash away the memory with cleansing tears.

Although she hadn't spoken directly to Garrett, Darcy Connor had suddenly discovered numerous reasons to call. The woman was obviously checking on Arden and the baby and making covert reports.

"Knock, knock." Layla stood in the doorway. As the teenage girls had happily announced, today had been an early release day for local schools. "This is an intervention."

"What?"

"Today, we close the studio early, go to your place and eat chocolate-covered caramels while we watch action movies with lots of car chases and explosions. Then, tomorrow, you start shaking this off, or I think your brothers are taking a road trip to the Double F and doing some damage. You remember your brothers, right? Big strapping guys who love you and are worried sick?"

"I'm not trying to worry any of you," Arden said apologetically. "I just…hurt."

"Oh, sweetie." Layla came around the desk to give her a hug. Then she pulled a caramel-filled chocolate medallion out of her pocket. "Here, want to get a jump start on the gorging?"

"No." Arden swatted the candy away. It made her

think of Garrett. *Big surprise.* Everything made her think of Garrett.

"If you miss him so much, you could call him."

"And say what? Layla, the guy expected me to marry him without ever mentioning his feelings for me. He thinks it's rational to get married for the baby's sake, and, you know what? He may be right. There are probably people who do that and make it work. But I'm holding out for more than *rational*. He made it sound like a good mother would want her child to have a loving home with both parents, and I *do*. Enough that I'm willing to wait for the right situation, for a man who actually does love me. A man who gives his future with me the due consideration it deserves. I can't just pack up and leave Cielo Peak!"

Layla narrowed her eyes at her, lips pursed.

"What?"

"Don't scream at me…but are you *sure* you can't?"

"Hey! You're one of the reasons I'm staying. Do you want to get rid of me?"

"What I want is to see you happy. I know we couldn't go out for spur-of-the-moment pizzas if you left, but even living in the same town, we spend half our time on the phone. You'd be moving to a ranch, not the far side of the moon."

"I have a business I started from scratch. And the thought of leaving my brothers…"

"Maybe you'd be setting a good example for them," Layla suggested quietly. "Colin can't seem to find his way back to happiness, and Justin is too afraid of being happy to give it a fair shot. If you seized happiness with Garrett, it could give them hope, a blueprint to follow.

I agree the man's proposal sucked, but let's look past that for the moment. Do you think he could make you happy?"

Arden stared into space, recounting all the small and not-so-small ways he'd done just that, the unexpected joy he'd given her.

"C'mon, you can think it over on the ride to your house." Layla had already picked up Arden's purse and was bringing the red wool coat to her. "You said Garrett goes in for testing next week? Maybe you can call him Sunday night, after you've both had a chance to calm down and reflect. Wish him luck on the medical stuff and see how you feel talking to him."

Conjuring a ghost of a smile, Arden stood. "You're a very wise woman."

"That's what I tell my students. Let's go. Bad action movies await."

"I don't think so." Arden gasped, gripping the edge of her desk. "My water just broke!"

ALL THE OTHER ranch hands had called it a day. Garrett should, too. It was cold and dark. But where else would he go? His house was too quiet, too lonely. And up at his parents' house, Caroline's admission seemed to have brought her and Brandon even closer. With the weight of her secret lifted, Caroline was practically giddy. She danced around the kitchen to her old records while baking, a constant smile on her face. The house was full of the cinnamon-spiced aroma of pumpkin pie and happiness.

He'd rather be out shivering in the barn.

The cell phone in his pocket rang, and he had to remove one glove to answer it. He almost ignored the call since he didn't recognize the number. "Garrett Frost," he announced himself.

"Frost? This is Justin Cade."

Garrett groaned. Was the man planning to kick Garrett's ass because he'd displeased Arden? "Look, if you're calling to bust my chops, you should know I *tried* to do the honorable thing."

"I'm calling because she's in the hospital." The swaggering man had never sounded so fragile. "How soon can you get here?"

BY THE TIME he reached the hospital, it was all over. Garrett was ravaged with self-blame. Why hadn't he been here with her? Had this happened because they'd had sex? Between all the machines in the hospital interfering with cell phone reception and Garrett driving through several "dead spots," he hadn't been able to stay in constant contact with Justin. Those moments of not knowing what was happening had been sheer hell.

What he did know was that Arden's membranes had ruptured a month too early. The doctors had given her antibiotics and had considered a drug to discourage labor as well as steroids to help speed development of the baby's premature lungs. But ultimately they'd decided the safest thing for both mother and child was an emergency C-section.

When he'd last spoken to Justin, that was all the man had known. Garrett burst into the maternity waiting room, frantic. Layla rose from a chair and ran to hug him.

"Tell me she's okay," he implored.

She nodded. "With the type of C-section they did, they had to knock her out. She's still asleep, but she should be fine. The baby was having a little bit of trouble breathing on her own, but she's on a ventilator in the NICU and—"

"She?" Garrett grabbed Layla's shoulders. The errant tears he'd fought since he'd jumped into his truck spilled over unchecked. "I have a daughter?"

Layla nodded emphatically. "Four pounds even. Name yet to be determined. Come on, her uncles are already upstairs watching her through windows."

Four pounds? Lord, she was smaller than a bowling ball but already had so many people in her life who already loved her. He followed Layla to the elevator bank. Now that the adrenaline in his body was starting to ebb, his legs felt too rubbery to take the stairs. The doors parted, and he was about to step inside the elevator when a nurse behind them called, "Family and friends of Arden Cade?"

He spun around. "Is she awake? Is she all right? Can I see her?"

The woman lowered her clipboard and gave him a patient smile. "Slow down there, sir. She's awake, but groggy. She'll experience some discomfort over her recovery period, but right now she's on some pretty strong painkillers. And, yes, you can see her. Only one at a time in the room until she's had a bit more rest."

"I'll go tell the guys." Layla squeezed his arm. "You tell Arden we all love her."

We all love her. God, he'd been an idiot. Why hadn't he dropped to one knee the last time he'd been with her, told her he'd never felt this way about another woman and begged her to marry him? He'd been cynical lately about matrimony and fidelity and honesty, but was that the kind of world he wanted to raise his daughter in? A place where people saw the worst in each other and didn't take risks with their hearts?

The nurse led him to a dimly lit maternity suite with a couple of guest chairs and a hospital bed angled so that Arden was reclining but not flat on her back. She was connected by IV to several different apparatuses and monitors. Wearing an unflattering hospital gown, tubes sticking out of her arms, plastic bracelets encircling her wrists, her damp hair sticking to a face bloated with the fluids they'd given her, she was easily the most beautiful woman he'd ever seen.

She blinked in confusion, as if trying to decide whether she was dreaming. "Garrett?" Her voice was slurred. "That you?"

"It's me." He came to her side, wondering if she'd let him hold her hand. Unable to stop himself, he leaned down to kiss her forehead. "Congratulations, I understand you have a beautiful daughter. But no way is she as beautiful as her momma."

"I need to hold her!" Splotches of color rose in her cheeks. "They put me under, I only glimpsed the hospital blanket and a blur and—"

"The nurse who brought me in here said they'll wheel you upstairs soon. They need to check some vitals first."

That seemed to calm her. She swallowed audibly, the sound dry and cracked, and he looked around for a pitcher of water.

"How'd you get here so fast?" she asked.

Fast? Under other circumstances, he would have

laughed at the irony. "Sweetheart, those were the slowest, most agonizing hours of my entire life. I felt like I was stuck in another dimension and couldn't reach you. It was a living nightmare."

Her eyes slid closed once again. "You're here now."

AFTER A NIGHT that passed in a fragmented series of narcotic impressions, Arden woke the next morning with a sense of awe. *I have a baby girl.* It seemed almost a dream, except for the pain in her midsection and the still-vivid memory of the fear she'd felt when the doctor had said they needed to do an emergency Caesarean.

Trying to remember how much of what she recalled was real, she turned her head to identify the source of snoring. She half expected to see Justin or Colin, but it was Garrett, his jaw covered in stubble, his legs hanging off a chair that transitioned into a twin bed about a foot too small for him.

"Garrett?"

He came awake immediately, his expression as chagrined as if he'd fallen asleep while he was supposed to be keeping watch. "I only closed my eyes for a minute."

She started to chuckle, but it hurt, tugging her insides in opposite directions. "You're allowed to sleep. How is she?"

"Healthy. She's upstairs in an incubator, but they say she's doing incredibly well for a preemie. She may have to stay in the hospital for a few weeks, but she should be home by Thanksgiving. My parents called about an hour ago. Would you mind if they come see you?"

"No, they should be here. Family's the most important thing in the world."

"Then you must be my family." He stood, coming to her side. "Because all I could think when I hauled ass to the hospital yesterday was that you're the most important thing in the world to me. You are my world. I'm sorry I didn't articulate that clearly enough until now."

She didn't know what to say. Could she trust what she was hearing, or were the drugs in the hospital very, *very* good?

"I can't wait to celebrate our first Thanksgiving as a family," he said. "And Christmas! I'll put so many lights on the outside of the house the baby thinks she lives in Times Square."

"You...sound like you plan to spend a lot of time at my house. Don't they need you at the ranch?"

"I don't want to be here just for your recovery— or hers, no matter how much I love her. I want you, Arden. If I have to, I'll ask Dad to give the foreman extra responsibilities, hire some extra help. I'll stay in Cielo Peak as long as you want. If you'll have me," he said brokenly.

"But the Double F—"

"What's one ranch compared to the entire world?"

"Arden, is this bum bothering you?" Justin's teasing voice came from the door, and Arden was glad to see his familiar face—although it looked as if it had gained several new worry lines in the past twenty-four hours.

"I'm not sure," Arden began, "but he *might* have been proposing."

"In a hospital room with no ring?" Justin snorted. "Frost, my sister deserves a string quartet and a five-star meal."

"As soon as she's all better and you volunteer to

babysit your niece, I'll take her out for those things. Right now, I'm improvising." He turned to Arden. "You asked me before why I wanted to marry you?"

She held her breath, almost afraid to hope.

He took her hand, his heart in his eyes. "Because I love you and always will."

"I love you, too." Joy filled her, and for a second she felt no pain at all. "And I'd like nothing more than to marry you."

Epilogue

Arden stood by her daughter's hospital crib, watching her sleep. "I hate that I'm going home without you, but I'll visit every day. And going home just means I can supervise Daddy while he gets your room set up perfectly," she whispered. "I'll tell you a secret, you've already got Daddy completely wrapped around your finger. Be careful with him. He may be a big, strong cowboy, but he's got a tender heart."

She couldn't believe he'd really been willing to move to Cielo Peak for them. She'd informed him that under no circumstances would she allow such a sacrifice. But they *would* have to remain for at least a few months, as their daughter got stronger. They'd relocate to the ranch sometime after New Year's and were hoping to get married around Valentine's Day.

Her husband-to-be was waiting for her in the hall, having already said his temporary goodbye to their daughter. As soon as the drugs had begun to wear off and Arden started having longer stretches of lucidity, Garrett had asked if she'd decided on a name for a baby. During her pregnancy, she'd toyed with the notion of perhaps naming a daughter for Natalie. Or after her own mother. But those both felt off the mark now. There was nothing wrong with honoring the past, but Arden wanted to focus on the bright, bright future ahead of them. They'd christened their daughter Hope.

"Everyone's waiting downstairs," he told her, putting his arm around her shoulders. "If you want to change your mind, I can tell Mom that—"

"No, we agreed. Caro's going to stay with me while you finally get that testing done. You already had to postpone because of me. I don't want this hanging over your head, Garrett. The nurses are giving Hope the best care possible, and you know your mom will look after me and call you with daily—possibly hourly—updates."

"I just hate to leave you."

"I know, but we have a whole lifetime ahead of us. We can spare a week of that to find out whether you can help Will."

During the days she'd been in the hospital, Garrett had told her all about how Brandon had forgiven his wife's transgression. And Arden had thought about the many rich blessings she and Garrett shared. If they could bless someone else with a second chance…

Even though she was able to walk by herself, hospital policy dictated that she be taken to the exit in a wheelchair. Apparently, there was a waiting list for the chairs, because the nurse who said she'd be right back had yet to reappear. The elevator doors parted, but it wasn't the nurse who stepped off the conveyance. Both her brothers were loaded down with her belongings, ready to take them to Garrett's truck, and they were accompanied by Layla and the Frosts.

"We just wanted one last peek at Hope through the window before we go," Layla said sheepishly. "I can't wait until you can bring her home, and I get to hold her as much as I want."

"Sorry, honey," Caroline said. "I've got grandmother's prerogative. You'll have to wait in line."

"Her parents get first dibs," Garrett said firmly.

Affection and gratitude filled Arden. How was it possible she had ever felt alone? She looked from the group assembled in the hall back to her beautiful daughter, then up into the eyes of the man who loved her. *My family.* Hope didn't know it yet, but they were the luckiest two ladies in all of Colorado.

* * * * *

*Be sure to look for the second book
in Tanya Michaels's
THE COLORADO CADES trilogy—
SECOND CHANCE CHRISTMAS.
Available in December 2013!*

REQUEST YOUR FREE BOOKS!
2 FREE NOVELS PLUS 2 FREE GIFTS!

HARLEQUIN®
American ★ Romance®
LOVE, HOME & HAPPINESS

YES! Please send me 2 FREE Harlequin® American Romance® novels and my 2 FREE gifts (gifts are worth about $10). After receiving them, if I don't wish to receive any more books, I can return the shipping statement marked "cancel." If I don't cancel, I will receive 4 brand-new novels every month and be billed just $4.74 per book in the U.S. or $5.24 per book in Canada. That's a savings of at least 14% off the cover price! It's quite a bargain! Shipping and handling is just 50¢ per book in the U.S. and 75¢ per book in Canada.* I understand that accepting the 2 free books and gifts places me under no obligation to buy anything. I can always return a shipment and cancel at any time. Even if I never buy another book, the two free books and gifts are mine to keep forever.

154/354 HDN F4YN

Name _____ (PLEASE PRINT) _____

Address _____ Apt. # _____

City _____ State/Prov. _____ Zip/Postal Code _____

Signature (if under 18, a parent or guardian must sign) _____

Mail to the Harlequin® Reader Service:
IN U.S.A.: P.O. Box 1867, Buffalo, NY 14240-1867
IN CANADA: P.O. Box 609, Fort Erie, Ontario L2A 5X3

Want to try two free books from another line?
Call 1-800-873-8635 or visit www.ReaderService.com.

* Terms and prices subject to change without notice. Prices do not include applicable taxes. Sales tax applicable in N.Y. Canadian residents will be charged applicable taxes. Offer not valid in Quebec. This offer is limited to one order per household. Not valid for current subscribers to Harlequin American Romance books. All orders subject to credit approval. Credit or debit balances in a customer's account(s) may be offset by any other outstanding balance owed by or to the customer. Please allow 4 to 6 weeks for delivery. Offer available while quantities last.

HAR13R

Check out this excerpt from
CALLAHAN COWBOY TRIPLETS
by Tina Leonard,
coming September 2013.

Tighe, the wildest of the Callahan brothers, is determined
to have his eight seconds of glory in the bull-riding ring—
but gorgeous River Martin throws off his game!

Tighe Callahan sized up the enormous spotted bull. "Hello, Firefreak," he said. "You may have bested my twin, Dante, but I aim to ride you until you're soft as glove leather. Gonna retire you to the kiddie rides."

The legendary rank bull snorted a heavy breath his way, daring him.

"You're crazy, Tighe," his brother Jace said. "I'm telling you, that one wants to kill you."

"Feeling's mutual." Tighe grinned and knocked on the wall of the pen that held the bull. "If Dante stayed on him for five seconds, I ought to at least go ten."

Jace looked at Tighe doubtfully. "Sure. You can do it. Whatever." He glanced around. "I think I'll go get some popcorn and find a pretty girl to share it with. You and Firefreak just go ahead and chat about life. May be a one-sided conversation, but those are your favorite, anyway."

Jace wandered off. Tighe studied the bull, who never broke eye contact with him, his gaze wise with the scores of cowboys whom he'd mercilessly tossed, earning himself a legendary status.

"Hi, Tighe," River Martin said, and Tighe felt his heart start to palpitate. Here was his dream, his unattainable brunette princess—smiling at him as sweet as cherry wine. "We heard you're going to ride a bull tomorrow, so the girls and I decided to come out and watch."

This wasn't good. A man didn't need his concentration wrecked by a gorgeous female—nor did he want said gorgeous, unattainable female to see him get squashed by a few tons of angry luggage with horns.

But River was smiling at him with her teasing eyes, so all Tighe could say was, "Nice of you ladies to come out."

River said, "Good luck," and Tighe shivered, because he did believe in magic and luck and everything spiritual. And any superstitious man knew it was taunting the devil himself to wish a man good luck when the challenge he faced in the ring was nothing compared to the real challenge: forcing himself to look into a woman's sexy gaze and not drown.

He was drowning, and he had been for oh, so long.

Look for CALLAHAN COWBOY TRIPLETS
by Tina Leonard, coming September 2013, only from
Harlequin® American Romance®.

SADDLE UP AND READ 'EM!

Looking for another great Western read? Check out these September reads from HOME & FAMILY category!

CALLAHAN COWBOY TRIPLETS by Tina Leonard
Callahan Cowboys
Harlequin American Romance

HAVING THE COWBOY'S BABY by Trish Milburn
Blue Falls, Texas
Harlequin American Romance

HOME TO WYOMING by Rebecca Winters
Daddy Dude Ranch
Harlequin American Romance

*Look for these great Western reads and more
available wherever books are sold or visit*
www.Harlequin.com/Westerns

A Navy SEAL's Surprise Baby

by

LAURA MARIE ALTOM

Fatherhood is the last thing on navy SEAL Calder Remington's mind. On the job, he's a hardworking hero; in civilian life, he's a carefree bachelor. When he finds a baby—*his* baby—on his doorstep, he's got no choice but to be a dad. He needs help, and that's where supernanny Pandora Moore comes in. She's perfect in every way and Calder can't deny that he's attracted to her. But Calder can't help wondering if she's hiding something. He never imagines that the truth may tear them apart—just as they dare to imagine a future together.

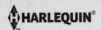

American Romance®

There's just something about a cowboy....

Skyler Harrington is a planner. After the tumult of her childhood, she's built a life for herself in Blue Falls, Texas, that's comfortable, predictable, safe. The last thing she needs is to go gaga over a rodeo cowboy. It felt great to let her hair down with sexy Logan Bradshaw, but she'll be happy if their paths never cross again.

A surprise pregnancy is something neither expected. She's willing to raise their child alone, but Logan is determined to prove he's more than a devil-may-care risk taker. He's daddy material!

Don't miss

Having the Cowboy's Baby

by TRISH MILBURN

Available September 3, only from Harlequin® American Romance®.